ARÍEL'S JOURNEY

THE ICE HORSE ADVENTURES

Ariel's Journey
The Ice Horse Adventures – Book #1
Copyright © 2008 by Doug Kane and Christy Wood

All rights reserved. Published by:

Blue Ink Press, Ltd.
Amherst, Ohio – Salem, Oregon

Cover and Book Design by Gwyn Kennedy Snider

Blue Ink Press
1246 Park Ave.
Amherst, OH 44001

ISBN 13: 978-0-9817234-0-2

Printed in Canada

www.Icehorseadventures.com

DOUG KANE AND CHRISTY WOOD

ARÍEL'S JOURNEY

THE
ICE HORSE
ADVENTURES
BOOK 1

Blue Ink Press, Ltd.

For Rory, Jan and Gigja
and
A Special Prayer For Prinsessa and Skessa

CONTENTS

ICELANDIC GLOSSARY

Abel (ah-bell)— bishop of Hólar

Agnar (ahg-nar) — Icelandic warrior of Akureyri

Akureyri (ah-ku-reree)— Icelandic fishing village

Angur (ahn-ger)— Icelandic horse ridden by Reynir

Ari (ah-ree)— Miller family Icelandic gelding

Aríel (ah-ree-al)— Miller family Icelandic mare

Arnþor (ahrn-thor)— Icelandic chieftain of Hólar

Baldur (bal-do-er)— Icelandic son of Máttur and Daria

Brynja (bree-n-yah)— Icelandic servant boy of Arnþor

Daria (dar-ee-ah)— Wife of Máttur and hostess to American girls

Drasill (drah-sitl)— Miller family Icelandic gelding

Fálki (fall-kee)— Miller family Icelandic gelding

Frami (fram-ay)— Icelandic villager of Hólar

Fina (feen-ah)— Miller family Icelandic mare

Freysteinn (grey-stahn)— bishop of Akureyri

Sleipnir (sleep-ner)— Eight-legged horse of the God Óðinn

Gelmir (gel-meer)— Miller family Icelandic gelding

Gígja (gee-yah)— Icelandic daughter of chieftain Arnþor

Hólar (hoe-lar)— Icelandic farming village

Hornafjörður (horn-ah-fay-yur-ther)— breed of Icelandic horse

Hela (hay-lah)— Miller family Icelandic mare

Hersir (her-seer)— Miller family Icelandic stallion

Kafteinn (kahf-tayn)— Icelandic stallion and head of Hólar herd

Kedja (keth-yah)— Miller family Icelandic mare

Kleinur (clay-newer)— Icelandic treat, similar to doughnuts

Laufabrauð (loy-vah-by-th)— deep fried Icelandic bread

Leifur (lay-vour)— Icelandic son of Máttur and Daria

Máttur (mah-toor)— husband of Daria and host of American girls

Prinsessa (prin-ses-ah)— Miller family Icelandic mare

Reynir (ray-kneer)— teenage Icelandic guide

Siklingur (sick-ling-ger)— Icelandic chieftain of Akureyri

Skessa (skess-ah)— Miller family Icelandic mare

Svaðastaðir (svah-thah-stah-ther)— breed of Icelandic horse

Tafar (tah-far)— Icelandic warrior of Arnþor

Torfi (tor-vay)— Icelandic villager of Hólar

Tjörvi (tyor-vee)— Icelandic warrior of Akureyri

Torfason (tor-vah-son)— Reynir's last name

Tölt (toh-lt)— famous Icelandic horse gait

Végeir (vee-ah-gah-er)— Icelandic servant of Arnþor

~ ONE ~

Horse Magic

My jeans are trashed! Look at this rip! I knew we should have changed first!" Kim sat on the ground examining the knee of her jeans, while Darcy tried to hold back her laughter. The horses approached the twelve-year-old girls eagerly, eyeing their bulging pockets, full of baby carrots. Whenever Darcy came to visit the Millers' farm, much of their time was spent with the herd of Icelandic horses that Kim's family raised. She had horses of her own, but the stocky, fluffy "Iceys" captured Darcy's heart the very first time she met them.

"Okay, I would have a little tiny bit of sympathy for you, except racing was your idea, even though you knew in your heart you were going to lose." Darcy's sense of humor came to life when she was with Kim. At school she was very shy, but here she could be herself. Horses were her passion, and when the Millers joined her 4-H group, Darcy and Kim became best friends in no time.

1

She stepped out of the way as Kim halfheartedly tossed a clump of grass at her. Darcy and Kim fed the horses their carrot treats and smoothed their hands over the wildly thick manes of the horses. When they'd eaten every carrot and had enough attention, the horses moved toward the hay bale thirty feet away.

"Hey! How'd you guys get down here so fast?" Emily, Kim's fourteen-year-old sister, joined the girls at the fence. Her wavy red-gold hair hung down her back and shone in the afternoon sun.

"Hi, Emily. I couldn't resist saying hello to the horses, and Kim decided it was a good time to shred her favorite jeans, right, Speedy?" Darcy grinned as Kim stuck her tongue out at her pal.

"Oh, Kim! You really did a number on those! You should have changed clothes before you came down to the barn."

"I know. But the horses were calling to us, seriously," Kim's green eyes twinkled as she teased her older sister.

"Alright, alright. You're going to have to patch them up and call them barn pants, I guess. Too bad we don't have Rosalie with us anymore—she'd fix them right up!"

"Well, that makes no sense, Em. If Rosalie was with us, we'd still be in the city—and we certainly wouldn't be hanging out with horses in our own yard!" The Millers' former life in Philadelphia was only twenty-five miles in distance, but it seemed a lot farther away.

"Wait a minute," Darcy interrupted, "Who's Rosalie?"

"She was our nanny 'slash' housekeeper when we lived in Philly.

She was practically family when Mom and Dad were working constantly," Emily explained.

"I can hardly even remember that life," Kim reflected as she pushed her bangs out of her eyes, "We're all so much happier here." The girls leaned against the white vinyl fence, watching the small herd of horses and foals nibble sweet smelling hay from the huge, round bale.

"You had a nanny and everything? No way! How did your family get out here?"

"Truth?" Emily glanced over her shoulder as if a spy could be hiding behind the oak trees. "If we had stayed there, Mom and Dad would have gotten divorced. They didn't even like each other any more. Mom was always worried about problems with her patient, or the hospital, or insurance companies, stuff like that. Dad was always yelling about some dumb client he was doing a trial for, or his partners or something. They both had their own problems, and I think they just took their frustrations out on each other."

Kim listened as closely as Darcy—she was only seven when their family moved, so she wasn't as aware of the situation. She tried to keep still, but the jingling of the two silver bracelets on her arm made a small ping ping noise as they hit the fence. The horses looked over at the noise for a moment, then went back to their snack.

"How bad was it, really?" Darcy wondered. "Do you think they could go from being that miserable to perfectly happy, just because they moved here? Lansdale's not paradise, you know!"

"It was much more than just the move. I mean, the quiet and being closer to nature—seeing stars at night and stuff like that—is great; but the magic came from the horses. Mom and Dad both fell in love with them and it was like they had joined this secret club. They were constantly talking about the Iceys, studying everything they could find. It was like they were gonna build their own 'Icey Lovers' tree house or something!"

"You know," added Kim, "I do remember that. They went from either not talking at all or arguing constantly, to giggling like kids planning a birthday party."

"Yeah, and things just kept rolling along, and here we are!"

"You know what I don't get?," Kim confided, leaning forward to hang over the fence and letting her ponytail flip forward, "when Mom was our age, she said she used to ride 'tall horses' like the 4-H gang and the Equestrian Youth Group members. What made her decide on Icelandic horses? They sure aren't anything like the tall horses, not that I'm complaining."

"It was definitely Prinsessa," Emily stated, smiling at the small bay mare with the huge mane and forelock, the queen of the herd, a total Alpha mare. "It was that trip to Virginia when we visited the Trimbles' farm. That's where Mom fell in love with Prinsessa and the Icelandic breed. I guess she was the snowball that started the avalanche."

"Yeah," Kim smiled with satisfaction. "And now she's mine."

"Yep. Remember when we brought Prinsessa home and a month later Aríel was born?" Emily reminisced. "Mom and Dad didn't even know she was pregnant! She's such a little chub that she always looks pregnant."

"Hey, don't talk about Prinsessa like that! She's royalty! And she can hear you, so watch your mouth," Kim grinned at Darcy as she straightened Emily out.

"Sorry," Emily smiled. "She may be shaped like a barrel, but she's still the perfect horse. Anyway, it didn't matter; Mom and Dad were so in love with Prinsessa and Aríel and Iceys in general that it didn't take Mom long to convince Dad that they should start a hobby farm to breed Icelandic horses. Remember all that research they did? Then when they traveled around to other Icelandic farms they figured out in a hurry that these little horses are easy to keep and the best trail horses in the world."

"Not just trail horses," Kim interrupted, "what about jumping and barrel racing and dressage and gaited horse shows and the county fair and, and…"

"You're right, you're right," Emily agreed, "which is why Mom and Dad bought Hersir, Skessa, and Hela from the Trimbles. It wasn't long before Fina and Ari were born. Then Mom and Dad had an Icelandic breeding business, and boy, were they lucky in their choices! Hersir has turned out to be the best little stallion in the world and all the babies have been perfect." Emily beamed at the horses with pride.

"Wow, it's so romantic, in a horse kind of way," Darcy mused. "Why'd you get all these other ones? Drasill, Gelmir, Fálki, and Kedja have been here since last spring, right?"

"Two points to Darcy for remembering all their names!" joked Emily. "Mom and Dad realized that some people were willing to buy fully trained, imported adult horses, even if they are pretty expensive. But it takes a whole year to get used to our environment and teach them the way we like to ride, which is why we still have them. They got Kedja because she was a champion in Iceland, like Hersir, and they wanted another mare to breed. Plus, Dad wanted a horse to ride."

"Yeah, but then how come Mom's the one who rides Kedja, who's tall, and Dad rides Hela, who's short and always stops to eat grass at the side of the trail?" Kim laughed. "Dad gets so annoyed when she does that. It's funny!"

"Well, Mom's a great rider and Kedja's a champion mare. Dad just learned to ride and even though Hela gives him a hard time, she's still an easy horse to ride. Dad loves her, even when she misbehaves. She just likes to see what she can get away with."

"I love it when the babies are born, but I'm always sad when we have to sell them," Kim said mournfully, hanging by one foot off the fence, practicing one of her old gymnastic moves.

"I know, silly." Emily tapped Kim on the arm lightly. "But if all we did was breed and import, but never sold any, we'd run out of space and it sure wouldn't be much of a business. Besides, they would never sell Hersir, Prinsessa, Skessa, Kedja, Hela, or Aríel—they're our horses."

"We better get in and start our homework before dinner," Emily announced, sounding more than just two years older than her younger sister. There were only a few school days left and then they would have the whole summer to enjoy riding, preparations for the county fair, and 4-H work nights. The girls were counting down the days to freedom. Until then, the Miller girls had to stick to their after-school routine.

The trio strolled up to the house, unaware that two of the horses had left their spot at the hay bale. Prinsessa and her daughter, Aríel, watched the trio for a few seconds, then turned to face each other. Aríel bobbed her head up, then down, and headed for the pasture. Prinsessa stayed in place until the three girls were out of her sight.

Supper was an event, with the three girls sharing their summer dreams with Mr. and Mrs. Miller. Karen Miller smiled as she watched the children enjoying the steamed broccoli, marinated chicken breasts, green salad, and corn muffins.

"Thank you, ladies, for making these muffins when you got home. They add so much to the meal."

"You're welcome," Emily gladly took credit for her idea. "But let's get back to the summer plans…what do you think? Are we ready to go camping this summer?"

"We'll talk about it," her father answered. But his wink at Kim told the girls it was a good possibility.

Giddy about the summer opportunities just around the corner, Darcy and Kim ran upstairs to the younger Miller's bedroom. Emily claimed dibs on the computer and dashed into the upstairs office.

~ TWO ~

A Challenge Is Established

Spreading nail polish, cotton balls, and tiny stickers out on her desk, Kim wondered aloud about 4-H work night. The work nights of the season started in the spring and prepared horses and riders for the upcoming summer competitions. Winter was filled with fundraising events and social activities, but the members and their horses enjoyed the practice sessions the most.

"I am so glad we are back into work nights! Winter lasted way too long, and I swear the horses knew when we go to 4-H without them."

"Yeah, they know all right! I felt so guilty not bringing the horses to meetings and the winter events. Movie night would have been more fun on horseback, you gotta admit."

"Ha! They'd eat all the popcorn, so I'm glad they stayed home!" Kim chose a bright pink shade for her toenails, and a clear coat for her fingernails. "My favorite night was the Chili Cook-Off, hands down. The fire extinguisher centerpieces were so fun to make, and that picture of all the cooks with their fireman hats on—that's a classic!"

Darcy shook the bottle of lavender polish and smiled. "When Mr. Sutton mixed up the 'Mellow & Mild' sign with the 'Viciously Spicy' sign, I thought smoke was going to actually come out of my dad's nose!"

"Don't make me laugh, I'm gonna smudge! How about when everybody found out the secret ingredient in Mrs. Gerlach's chili?"

Darcy and Kim squealed together, "Peanut butter!"

"I don't even care, it was delicious. Mrs. McClain's did deserve to win, though, because it took her a week to make it."

"Well, I just want to know what you could possibly do to chili for a week—I think her son made that up."

"No way, Ian's too cute to lie."

Emily interrupted the spa treatment and gossip session when she came tiptoeing into Kim's room. "Hey, you two. Getting gorgeous for tomorrow's work night?"

"Maybe. Although natural beauty doesn't need any help."

"Yeah, right…in that case, put on two coats," Emily ducked when Kim tossed a pillow at her head. She plopped onto the bed.

"Were you IM-ing?" Darcy asked.

"Yeah, and listening to some music. The weirdest thing happened though. You are not going to believe it. I tried calling Laura, but she's on dinner duty," Emily rolled her eyes. "Her mom makes a two hour extravaganza out of dinner, so her phone's still off."

As if on cue, Emily's cell phone began chirping.

"Oh man, this is gonna be Laura. I'll put her on speakerphone. Sh-h! And not a word to Mom, under penalty of death."

Darcy and Kim exchanged wide-eyed looks as Emily set the phone in the middle of the bed and pushed the speakerphone button.

"Hi Laura! Finally! I have you on speakerphone so Kim and Darcy can hear this."

"Hey, girls! This must be big."

"It is, believe me. And it's about the Iceys, so it affects us all. And Laura, FYI, your mom is a dinnertime drill sergeant! Your phone's been off for two hours!"

"We're not pushing away the feed bag around here, not on spaghetti night! I'm totally stuffed. Now what's so big? I got your message the minute I turned my phone back on!"

"Okay, I cannot believe you were slurping noodles while I was in a major crisis, but I think I've been challenged to a duel…well, Skessa was, really. But I accepted on her behalf."

"Hello? Wait a minute! Did I get a wrong number? Are you sure this is Emily Rose Miller's phone? Did you just fall down the stairs? Get kicked in the head, maybe?"

"Stop it! This is serious! And it's totally not my fault. There I

11

was, minding my own business and my IM pops up. It's Andrea."

"I thought you were gonna block her?"

"I was, but my mom would give me the whole 'be the better person' and '4-H is a team, you are a player among players' lecture."

"True. Okay, so the RCG queen IM's you...go on..."

"So we're talking about school or whatever, and I knew she was gonna pull something. And I think the other two Red Carpet Girls were over there."

"Well, duh! They never go anywhere without all three. Sorry, proceed."

"Hold it. Laura, this is Darcy. What's RCG's? Who are the carpet girls?"

Emily blushed as she explained, "RCG stands for Red Carpet Girls. Andrea and her little groupies always strut around school like they're on the red carpet at an awards show—posing for their fans and the paparazzi. Madison thought of that at our last sleepover, didn't she?"

"Yep, it was Madison, definitely. Go on..."

"Okay, so I was playing along all nice...then Andrea asked me if I'd teach her to draw Icelandic horses, since they're so different from REAL horses. She said she just can't get them short and chubby enough, they always turn out looking like...get this... pigs."

"No way! She did not say that! She is gonna drown next time it rains, her nose is so high up in the air..."

"Yeah, she said it—all sweet and sugary and 'no offense, of course,' but she knew what she was saying."

"What did you do? You told her off, right? Blasted her?"

"Yeah, I'm gonna blast her and then have her print it for her mommy...that would be brilliant! No, I just told her I'd see her at work night and I hoped she had a great practice...and then she asked what was that supposed to mean..."

"Come on! This is great!"

"...so I said it wasn't supposed to mean anything, that she can take it however she wants...and then she said 'Meet me on the course at practice'...and I was, like, 'whatever, see you there.' So I guess we'll see if she shows up, right?"

"Wait a minute, hold on. She challenged you for tomorrow night?"

"I guess. Sorta weird, right? But I'm ready for her."

"Of course you're ready for her! It's about time you stood up to her. Oh this is too much. Have you told anyone else?"

"No! It's just you, me, Darcy, and Kim that know. Well, and Andrea...and maybe all the RCG's."

"Alright, we have got to keep this quiet. If you think your mom would get mad about you blocking Andrea's IM's, you do not want her getting the scoop on this. Don't say a word to anyone, got it?"

Emily signed off with Laura, while the younger girls stared at her in amazement. "No...way," was all Kim could say.

Darcy had a few questions. "How are you going to keep this quiet? Why did you agree to this? Is Skessa really up for this? What will your mom do if she finds out?"

After a few minutes, Emily headed over to her room and left the other two girls to their nail painting project. Before she left, she warned them both, especially Kim, to keep quiet about the 'one-on-one' coming up at work night.

Since it was a school night, Kim's mom insisted on an early bedtime. That way, she explained, they could still giggle and goof around for a while before conking out. The girls laughed themselves unconscious and hopped up when Kim's alarm rang in the morning. They headed out to tend to the horses, showered quickly, and came down for breakfast.

As the girls entered the sunny yellow kitchen in the beautiful old white farmhouse, their mother moved quickly to get cereal and lunches ready. She was wearing blue pants and a white blouse, looking like any typical mother. Once she got to the clinic, Dr. Karen Miller would don her white lab coat with the stethoscope hanging halfway out the pocket.

"Are you girls all ready for school? Are the horses fed?" She looked past the crisp, yellow-and-white-checked gingham curtains framing the kitchen window to the herd in the pasture and smiled contentedly as her daughters chimed, "Yes, Mother!"

"Don't forget, tonight is 4-H work night at the Klingshern's farm. We'll have to load up Prinsessa and Skessa on the trailer as soon as I get home from the clinic. I have patients until 4:30. Try to get a snack to hold you over until after 4-H."

Kim picked at her Raisin Bran. "Why do we get teased so much about our horses at work night and on trail rides?" Emily shot her a warning glance, but Kim continued.

Their mother didn't turn around but answered in a matter-of-fact tone. "People don't understand Icelandic horses, Kim. They think they're some kind of expensive, rare, exotic breed. It all comes down to envy. Just ignore it and try to have fun. Someday the other kids will figure out how great these little horses really are."

"I know, Mom," Kim lamented, "but it really stinks."

"Honey, the horses don't care. Anyone who really meets them falls head over heels in love—you know that." Dr. Miller ran her fingers through the top of Kim's hair and looked at her thoughtfully.

"Let me think about it," she told her younger daughter, pulling her tortoise shell framed glasses off her head, shoving them onto her face, and peering at the front page of the paper. "Maybe I can come up with something. Now, get eating, girls, so you don't miss your buses."

Emily's bus would come first, carrying her off to North Penn High School over in Lansdale, Pennsylvania; Kim and Darcy's would arrive a few minutes later, taking them about a mile north to Pennfield Middle School in nearby Hatfield.

The girls wolfed down their breakfast, grabbed their loaded

backpacks from the mudroom by the backdoor, and then rushed out to kiss Prinsessa and Skessa on their noses.

Hersir stood back a few steps, watching intently. Hela kept her head in the round bale, ignoring the whole scene. Skessa smeared a little muck on Emily's clean shirt. Emily brushed it off and ran for the school bus as it rumbled toward them down the country lane. Emily hopped off her bus and walked toward the entrance of the high school, alongside her friends Hayley Larson, Laura Westwood, and Madison Jacobs. Everyone chattered at the same time. All were equestrian fanatics and participated in 4-H and the Equestrian Youth Group. Emily and Kim had moved into the new school system when their family purchased what they now called Miller's Farm out on Schwab Road. Most of their friends had been born and raised in Lansdale, a small town located about twenty-five miles north of Philadelphia. Even though it was difficult to start over in a new school and make new friends, the fact that they shared a passion for horses bonded them quickly and the transition was a lot easier than Emily had expected.

"You don't really think you're going to win any ribbons at the fair with your fuzzy little ponies, do you?" Hayley teased, referring to the preparations at work night for the competitions at the fair.

"Hayley!" Emily huffed, exasperated. "You know perfectly well they are not ponies!"

"I know. I'm just teasing, Emily," Hayley replied, her eyes apologetic behind little round wire framed glasses. She was studious and quiet, but had a good sense of humor under a mop of brown curls that refused to be tamed no matter how many gels, straighteners, and mousses she glopped on it.

"I still don't get it, Emily." Laura was the prettiest of the four girls. She was tall and thin with long, thick blond hair and sapphire blue eyes. She carried herself with an air of maturity that made her seem older than fourteen. She leaned in front of Hayley toward Emily, her red backpack whacking Hayley's shoulder. "My pony, Flash, is almost a hand taller than Kedja, and she's the tallest horse in your herd."

"I just think the word 'pony' is totally relative. I've seen pretty tall POA's, and even if it means 'Pony of America', they are horses 'cause they can carry an adult and do what tall horses do. Same for our Iceys," Emily told her.

Madison appeared as delicate as a piece of fine china, but could dispel that by vigorously mucking out a stall in twenty minutes flat. She had been silent through the conversation, but finally broke in. "Well, I think they're all totally adorable, even if my Sam could jump over any one of them."

"Remember," Emily reminded Madison, "Skessa jumped the same height rail that Sam did and Sam's almost seventeen hands."

"Oh that's right! That was awesome!" Madison laughed and the dimple in her cheek appeared. "That was the highest rail I ever got Sam to jump."

The girls sat on a wall by the entrance, waiting for the bell to ring and fiddling with their cell phones, eventually turning them off so they wouldn't forget and have them confiscated in class.

The courtyard outside the school hummed with activity. Students congregated there, waiting until the last minute to enter the confining hallways. Clusters of teens chose their territory on the lawn or the sidewalk. Many of them had one ear bud dangling, one in their ear, so they wouldn't have to go without music or conversation. Cell phones rang and beeped as friends caught up on the news of the morning. Tough kids tossed their backpacks in a heap and posed, some leaning against the brick wall of the building. Pretty girls complimented each other's clothes and complained about their hair. A boy tossed his friend's backpack into a tree and heckled him while he climbed up to retrieve it. Chasing around the shrubs and laughing, a handful of boys flirted with girls who were pretending to ignore them. A group of shaggy-haired boys skateboarded off the steps and rails of the far entrance, their boards rolling and clicking loudly on the cement; scattered couples sat closely together, holding hands, kissing, or just leaning on each other. Car doors slammed as parents pulled in and out, dropping off their children.

Hayley, Laura, and Madison had been best friends since kindergarten and participated in just about any equestrian activity they could. None of them cared about the expensive tack and clothing that other parents bought. Nor did they have access to expensive trainers and instructors. Of the four families, Emily's was the only one who could afford the fancy paraphernalia, but her mother was vehemently against it. She believed that equestrian competitions and activities were about the rider and the horse, not the accessories.

Jim and Karen Miller had found a great instructor for the whole family. Carolyn Gray had been teaching for thirty years and had the same philosophy as Karen. Her teaching strategy was based on the philosophy that the best foundation, for any equestrian sport or activity was the basic riding skills of balance, posture, and good communication with the horse. Although Carolyn loved the Icelandics, she was very particular about her versatility and client base of many breeds. It was through lessons from Carolyn and research on the Internet that Jim and Karen had realized that the best way to raise Icelandics was to treat them as they did in Iceland. Typical American horses were kept in a stall and barely got fresh air or exercise, except for the hour or so a day when they were allowed to go outside. The Millers' horses stayed outside all year long, living in a herd, but had open stalls along the sides of the stable that they could use as shelter. Each stall had an automatic waterer, so with the use of round bales, the waterers, and the open shelter, the farm was one of the most efficient to operate in the area.

It was not just the farm that made it possible for the family to keep up their hobby business along with their incredibly busy jobs and schedules—it was the horses themselves. Jim and Karen learned early that with unlimited access to hay and water, continuous freedom of movement and herd life, their horses remained in the best state of health. The foals were born without human assistance, and the herd themselves managed the foals' education. This was one of the most amazing parts of breeding the Icelandics.

The foals attached themselves to the stallion within a few days of birth. Hersir was the best babysitter and teacher Karen had ever seen. She had never seen a stallion that cared for the babies as Hersir did. The foals stayed with Hersir more than with their mothers. Another amazing thing was the way Hersir's colts, which the Millers always gelded, became an important part of his herd. Unlike other breeds where a gelding could never be left with a stallion in a herd with mares, Hersir lived happily with his young colts, the mares, and foals all year long. Of course, Hersir's fillies and young mares had to be kept in a separate herd so no inbreeding would occur, but that herd was separated by only ten feet of walkway across the entire length of the pastures and Hersir still felt that both herds belonged to him.

Altogether, the Miller's farm was very low maintenance and produced some of the best Icelandic horses in the country. It was a lot to be proud of, and the family shared a strong bond with their horses.

"Oh, no! Here come the Red Carpet Girls. Spare me!" Hayley

groaned under her breath as three girls slid delicately out of a BMW sedan, looking around to see who was noticing their arrival at school. Madison chortled and made picture-snapping sounds. Dressed in skimpy designer clothes, with a book or two carried nonchalantly in one hand (versus the overloaded backpacks everyone else had), an iPod in the other and their cell phones clipped to their Gucci purses, they tossed their hair back and headed right toward Emily, Laura, Madison, and Hayley. These three girls coming at them, Andrea Norton, Heather Woodbridge and Erica McCarthy, were considered their greatest opponents and the most hostile adversaries in everything they did, especially in equestrian competitions.

They were kids who relied on money rather than skill to win ribbons and fame.

"Hi, girls! See you tonight," Andrea smirked down at Emily. "I see you're already dressed for work night—good thinking!" Her entourage waved as they passed, wiggling their fingers and squinting their eyes with exaggerated smiles, as if they were gesturing to a group of adoring fans.

"Yep, see you tonight," Emily said loftily, refusing to let Andrea provoke her. To her friends, she muttered, "Just because you spend mega-bucks on clothes, trainers, and tack, doesn't mean your horses are as good as ours." Then she glanced down at her simple cap-sleeve T-shirt, blue jeans, and gym shoes.

Madison and Hayley agreed, with comments of "Too bad money

can't buy her a brain!" and "Did you see the way she looked us up and down?" Laura, who had no patience for the Red Carpet Girls' attitudes and cattiness, stood up, gave Andrea, Heather, and Erica a withering look as she passed them, and went into the school. She refused to waste her time even listening to them.

"Can't we somehow kick them out of our 4-H chapter? They're an embarrassment!" Madison argued, her cheeks turning beet red. "How can their riding tack cost more than my horse?"

"Don't worry about it," Hayley said, "Maybe all three of them are going to move away."

"Really? What do you know that I don't know?" Madison demanded.

"Ha! Nothing, but I can dream, can't I?" Hayley shrugged at her pals as the morning bell rang and they headed to their lockers.

~ THREE ~

Trouble at Work Night

Later that afternoon, Kim hopped into the shiny aluminum stock trailer with Prinsessa walking behind at the end of a loose lead line. The horse walked up to the edge of the opening as if she were approaching a feed bowl. The little mare was so short that the trailer edge came halfway up her forelegs. Just as she reached the rubber edge, she paused for a millisecond, then suddenly rose up on her hind legs as if she was going to rear on Kim, but her front hooves only lifted a couple of feet in the air and then gently landed in the trailer. The mare took a few more steps behind Kim until her hind legs reached the edge. Then with another little hop, she was in and walking toward the front of the trailer.

Emily and Karen laughed. "Do you remember," Emily said, still giggling at Prinsessa's trailer entry, "the time we were cantering through the woods and Skessa made that giant leap over that huge log? Prinsessa ran up and first she hopped over it with her forelegs then walked up a couple feet and hopped over with her hind legs! That was the funniest thing I ever saw."

"Yeah," Kim replied a little defensively," but Prinsessa can take a barrel better than any horse in 4-H."

"We're not laughing at Prinsessa," said Karen, "we love her way too much. She is the best of the best. We just love her style of entering the trailer."

"Well," Kim said, still irritated, "you could have gotten a trailer with a shorter step."

"Besides," Karen added, "Prinsessa's body's just built that way. That's the shape she's supposed to be. She's beautiful the way she is, just like you girls. Everybody's different, and that's okay; we aren't supposed to all look the same."

Kim and Emily looked at each other and rolled their eyes. They'd heard this speech from their mother before about their bodies and the importance of good self-esteem; in Karen's family practice, she saw a lot of both obesity and anorexia among teenage girls.

"We know, Mom," Kim sighed in a long-suffering way.

"I'm just saying..."

"We know, Mom!" the girls chorused.

During their conversation, Prinsessa had turned around in the wide open stock trailer to dive into a flake of hay stashed on the floor for their trip. Kim was still standing next to Prinsessa when Emily hopped in and Skessa leaped in behind her as if she were in a jumping competition. With any other breed of horse, two horses loose in an open stock trailer with two girls could have been disastrous. But Skessa merely landed with a thump, walked behind Prinsessa, turned, nudged her pal with a friendly nod of the head and started eating off the same flake of hay. Once again the unique personalities of the Icelandic horses shone through. The two horses did not push or fight or dart for the door. They just calmly stood and ate while the girls unhooked their leads and jumped back out of the trailer.

Karen swung the huge door closed and latched it.

"Mom," Kim asked, "why does everyone else smoosh their horses into those tight little slots and tie them up so they can't even move their heads?"

Karen replied, "Well, the Iceys have extraordinary balance that other horses don't. Have you ever noticed how, given their freedom, they always stand backwards in the trailer?"

"Yeah," Kim's look was intent as she regarded her mother.

"That's because when the truck is braking," Emily interrupted, "it's a lot harder to keep your balance than when it is accelerating. When we stop for a light or something, the Iceys lean forward to keep their balance. We don't accelerate with as much force as when we brake."

"Good explanation, Em," Karen nodded with approval. "You've been paying attention in your physics class."

Emily laughed and they all climbed into the truck.

"Oh, I forgot my sunglasses. I'll be right back." Karen got back out and went into the house.

Kim leaned over to her sister and hissed in a loud whisper, "You better watch it, Em! The closer it gets, the worse your challenge against Andrea sounds. What if you get caught?"

"Oh relax! I shouldn't have even told you. It's just a friendly little face-off."

"Friendly? Yeah, right. Well, be careful, you know how Mom is about treating other people."

"Yeah, I know. It'll be fine. It's just a riding competition, that's all." Emily's eyes warned her little sister to drop the subject as their mother opened the truck door and got in, holding her sunglasses case. Karen picked up the conversation where she had left off.

"So, I was reading an article on the Internet that equestrian researchers did some studies and placed a bunch of horses from different breeds in the back of an open tractor trailer." Karen started the truck's ignition and carefully checked all her mirrors. "They drove the trailer for a while, then stopped and checked on the horses. You know what they found? That all the horses were all standing backwards. The researchers came to the conclusion that the horses were too busy trying to keep their balance to bicker or move around, and the part about standing backwards proved that they were intelligent enough to know which way to stand to make it easier to keep their balance."

"What about stopping suddenly or crashing?" Kim wanted to know.

"That's a completely different issue, Kimber. You can't cover everything."

Karen began to drive the big truck and trailer with ease, out the driveway and down the gravel lane, lined by a white rail fence. It was only about six miles to the Klingshern's farm. The area all around the Miller's farm and the Klingshern's farm was a good mixture of very expensive homes and horse farms, as well as middle-class homes and other farms, with other animals, cows, chickens, goats, and sheep. As they drove, the two girls chattered about 4-H, school, and the horses. Karen listened to their youthful talk, feeling blessed to have such bright, well-adjusted, friendly teenagers. She reminded herself to remember this moment when one of them was stressing her out later.

After about ten minutes, Kim turned to her mother and stated, "Our horses never bicker or fight."

Karen smiled to herself at the sudden change back to the earlier conversation.

"No, you're right, they don't," she responded. "And that's part of their personality that I think makes them so special."

Dr. Miller turned the truck into the Klingshern's driveway, maneuvering her way easily through the other trailers. She pulled the large rig between two other truck and trailer combinations in the dusty open field used for parking.

"Oh, good! Darcy's here!" Kim exclaimed, recognizing the silver and white horse trailer, which was parked nearby.

The late afternoon sun was still shining as the girls unloaded their tack and dumped it on the floor in the big arena. Then they ran over to their friends and started chattering away. Karen called them back and reminded them that they might need their horses. The whole group of girls ran for the trailer, without a break in their giggling conversations. Skessa and Prinsessa gently stepped down out of the trailer and followed the girls on a loose lead into the arena.

The Klingshern's farm was enormous; the beautiful stone farmhouse had been built in the early nineteenth century, but the stables, indoor and outdoor arenas, and pasture fencing were all relatively new and meticulously cared for. The wealthy Klingsherns bred and trained thoroughbreds for racing and were famous in thoroughbred circles. Their children were grown now, so they didn't participate in the 4-H activities, but were kind enough to lend the group their massive indoor and outdoor arenas for work nights.

The evening started out uneventfully. There were about thirty 4-H members and with some of the parents, plus the advisors, there were nearly fifty attendees at each work night. Fortunately, the Klingshern's arenas were set up for shows, with bleachers for parents and siblings to sit on along the sides of both the indoor and outdoor arenas. The kids tacked up and warmed up their mounts.

Each 4-H advisor worked with a group of six to eight boys and girls. The different groups were made up of teenagers who were designated to compete in a certain class or event at the county fair. The fair was held in late August and the groups had begun serious practice and training way back in March. During the winter, the groups focused on planning and fundraising.

After a half hour of warm-up, the riders broke up into their individual groups for lessons and practice. Kim was in barrel racing and Emily participated in jumping and dressage. Emily, Hayley, Laura, and Madison and their rivals, Andrea, Heather, and Erica were scattered among the different groups, but Andrea and Emily were both in the same classes. That was where the competition was the fiercest.

Andrea and Emily proceeded through their lessons without even looking at each other, but when it came time to practice, the fire between them began to smolder. In the outdoor arena, the Klingsherns had set up various jumps with rails at different levels. At the very end of the arena was the highest and most difficult jump. The practice began with riders beginning to jump at the height they were most comfortable with, then working their way up as high as they dared. Andrea's thoroughbred stood several hands taller than Skessa, but Skessa was far more powerful with her thick sturdy legs and broad muscular shoulders.

Andrea led the way, heading for a medium height jump. She sailed over it smoothly, grinning with a confident superiority.

As soon as the horse hit the ground, she turned, smoothing her expensive riding shirt with her left hand and headed for the next jump. Emily steered Skessa in behind Andrea and also took the jump with ease. With each jump, Emily moved up until she was alongside Andrea, and at one point the girls took a fairly high jump at the same time.

Meanwhile, murmured word of the escalating competition had spread through the groups inside the big arena. Many of the riders left off their practice and rode outside to watch the battle. Andrea's friends Heather and Erica leaned up against one section of the fence, reins grasped in one hand, and glared over at Laura and Madison, who were standing on the opposite side, watching Emily. Laura watched calmly, silently rooting for Emily, but Madison, nervous for her friend, bit her lip and clutched her reins so hard, her fingers turned white. The crowd of spectators had grown by the time the two girls took the jump together, and when Emily and Skessa hit the ground, Skessa took the lead with a huge leap. There weren't many more levels left. Emily saw out of the corner of her eye that the advisors, who had congregated over by the table that held coffee, water, and juices for a break, were beginning to notice what was going on. She also knew they would bring the competition to a stop. Quickly, she steered Skessa toward the end of the outdoor arena and the highest jump. Skessa was cantering with huge graceful lopes, while Andrea swatted Star with a crop, trying to push ahead. In a matter of seconds, Skessa had reached the approach to the jump and then she propelled herself over the rail, leaving a clearance of almost six inches.

"Good girl, Skessa," Emily murmured and Skessa's ears flickered. The spectators cheered and clapped, hollering, "Way to go, Emily!"

Andrea's brow creased in a frown and she felt herself flushing with anger. "That girl is not going to beat me," she muttered under her breath. At that point, she lost both her temper and control of her horse. The powerful gelding felt Andrea's balance shift, which threw off his gait. When it came time to make the jump, he nicked the rail with a front hoof, knocking it over. Star swerved as he landed, and Andrea fell to the soft arena footing in a heap.

Heather, leaning on the fence, immediately made a move to see if Andrea was hurt, but within a second Andrea leaped to her feet, her riding helmet knocked askew and her extravagant riding outfit covered with wood shavings. Star immediately recovered and came to a halt, standing quietly a few feet from the jump. Andrea didn't even glance at her horse, but took off after Emily and Skessa, furious. Emily was so proud, she walked Skessa casually back up the arena, unaware Andrea closing in behind her. Just as she came to a halt in front of the gate, listening to the cheers, Andrea ran up from behind, reached for Emily's belt and pulled her to the ground.

Several people watching gasped. Laura flung her riding helmet off, her long blond hair streaming out and made a move to spring like a wild cat. "Come on! Let's get out there and kick her butt!"

"No, Laura!" Madison reached over and grabbed Laura. "This is Emily's fight, not ours."

It took all of Laura's willpower to resist vaulting over the fence, but she knew Madison was right. She stood with her fists clenched and her body tensed.

Andrea tried to slam down onto Emily but Emily was too fast for her; with a quick spin and roll move, she was sitting on top of Andrea, pinning her hands on the ground beside her head.

"Get off me!" Andrea squirmed and twisted, furious. "Get off me now!"

"No! What are you doing—yanking me off Skessa like that? You say you're sorry!"

"No way, you skank!"

"Say it!"

"Girls! Girls! Stop this right now!" Two of the advisors grabbed the girls and pulled them apart, pulling Emily off Andrea and yanking Andrea to her feet. "Are you hurt? Are you hurt?" they asked.

The two girls, disheveled and glaring at each other chorused, "No, no," and pushed the advisors' hands away. Andrea immediately began straightening her designer riding clothing to some semblance of order and smoothing her hair. Emily just stood with her hands at her sides, breathing hard and staring at Andrea in disbelief.

Someone had gone to get Andrea's mother, Virginia, who

had sneaked out to have a cigarette behind her truck. She came running across the arena, her brassy bottle-blond hair in a messy pile atop her head. The forbidden and forgotten cigarette was still dangling from one hand, which was waving around spasmodically as she screamed at the top of her lungs, "What in God's name is going on? Who's attacking my daughter? Andrea, what did you do? Always getting into trouble! I can't leave you alone for two minutes!" She turned on Emily next. "Are you beating up my daughter?" Then she began yelling at the 4-H advisors. "Who's responsible for this? Why weren't you watching her? You're in charge!"

"Put that thing out, Mrs. Norton!" Rachel, one of the advisors, told Andrea's mother, disgusted. "You're going to drop some ash and burn this whole place down!"

Emily stepped away from the advisors and grabbed for Skessa's reins. She pulled her forward and gave her a big kiss on the nose. Skessa wasn't even breathing hard. Andrea threw herself into her mother's arms in typical dramatic fashion and burst into tears. Emily stood and listened, her face impassive as Mrs. Norton held her daughter and screamed at her over Andrea's wails.

"My daughter is an excellent rider and wonderful sportsman— woman. Obviously, this is your fault, this... this... unprovoked attack! We should sue! Are you hurt, dear? Did she injure you?" Mrs. Norton said in an aside to Andrea, but loud enough that everyone could hear her. "Look! Look at this! This other girl is completely fine and my own daughter is not! You're all witnesses!"

Almost all the people who had watched the incident rolled their eyes; they were witnesses and had seen Andrea's hysterics from start to finish.

Karen had been working with Kim's barrel racing team in the indoor arena when the ruckus started. She was at the opposite end of the indoor arena with a group of boys and girls about Kim's age. No one had noticed the movement to the large arena doors and when Karen heard the screaming coming from outside, she looked up in surprise at the empty arena. She turned to look at Kim, who looked back at her mother, her cheeks flushed. Karen knew Emily was up to something by the look on her younger daughter's face. She ran for the door.

Karen could not believe what she saw when she reached the group of advisors and parents who had congregated around the two girls, one horse and one screaming parent.

"Mrs. Norton! Mrs. Norton!" Rachel exclaimed, but Virginia ignored her and kept up her loud one-sided complaints. Andrea was wailing and Emily, looking a little the worse for wear, was stroking Skessa and whispering in her fuzzy ear. Karen marched up to her daughter and grabbed Emily by the arm.

"Come with me right this minute!" Karen excused herself to the other advisors and dragged Emily and Skessa out of the gate and over to their trailer. The second they reached the trailer, Kim rode up on Prinsessa.

"I do not know what in the world that was all about," Karen told Emily, her teeth clenched. "You will pack up your things. We will leave and we will be having a discussion. Once I get to the bottom of it, we will then take the appropriate steps to rectify this situation, whatever that may be. Do I make myself clear, Emily Louise Miller?"

"Yes, ma'am," Emily replied.

"Kimberly, get your things together and get Prinsessa loaded."

"Yes, Mother," Kim knew when her mother addressed her by her full name and in that tone, she should not say a word, even though she didn't have anything to do with what had happened.

By this time, it was beginning to get dark and, subdued by the commotion, practice and lessons were unofficially over for the evening. Most of the other riders began filtering out with their parents and packing up as Emily and Kim silently gathered their tack and loaded up Skessa and Prinsessa. They saw their friends, who knew better than to say anything, but waved and gave them sympathetic smiles from across the arena. Karen waited in the driver's seat, jaw set.

Pulling out of the Klingshern's driveway and onto the road, Karen gave a big sigh. "Emily, before I say anything, I want you to tell me honestly, exactly what happened out there. I don't want to hear that it wasn't your fault. There were two of you involved in that disgraceful scene and there's a reason why it was such a big deal. You can tell me what went on, but I also want you to spell out for me exactly what part was Andrea's fault and what part was your fault. Start talking."

Kim, who hated conflict of any kind and especially when it involved her sister, slid down in the seat, and stared out the truck window, her eyes barely high enough to see the deepening twilight and the serene farmland they were passing as the sky moved from lavender to purple.

Emily started by telling her mother about the jumps and the two of them competing and then how she got the higher one and how Andrea came after her and pulled her off Skessa and knocked her down. In the backseat, Kim gasped. Karen said nothing, but her eyes narrowed and her jaw tightened. She slowed down as a possum scrabbled across the road in front of the truck, its beady pink eyes eerie and luminous in the truck's headlights. Emily finished the explanation, including Mrs. Norton's hysterical accusations up to the part where Karen had come out.

"So now, tell me, what led up to this level of hostility between you two?" Karen wanted to know.

"Mom, Andrea and her friends are constantly giving us crap—"

"Please do not say crap; it's not a nice word respectable girls use—"

"—constantly giving us a hard time about the Iceys and talking down to us like we're a bunch of idiots. They think they're so much better because they spend all this money on their clothes and their riding gear and they act all uppity. Arguing with her and Heather and Erica is useless! Those girls are clueless and they're mean! When Andrea and I started jumping, I guess I just wanted to show her by action—not words—that I am a good rider and that Skessa is a great horse! I don't see what's so wrong with that."

"There are always going to be people like that, Emily, who think they're better than everyone and don't get much past the material things in life. You're right, you can't argue against that. But you've got to rise above it and just focus on what you're doing and not what someone else is thinking about you or Skessa! So I think you've told me what you think is Andrea's problem and why it's her fault. What part of that fight was your fault?"

Emily turned away from her mother and looked out the window for a few minutes. Karen waited patiently. Kim was anxious to hear what her sister would say and waited too, unconsciously holding her breath.

"I guess," Emily finally said, "because I knew I was better and I wanted to show her I was better, I showed her up in front of everyone and it hurt her pride. Instead of a legitimate competition, I made it personal. I shouldn't have done that, just to try to make myself feel better at her expense."

"That is some very good insight, Emily. You know, you don't have to care for every person you meet, but you have to learn the skills of how to get along with everyone. Plus, you don't know what problems Andrea has in her life. She might be envious of you, or have something going on at home that's not pleasant and she tries to act a certain way to feel more confident about herself."

"Or maybe she's just a jerk," Kim murmured from the backseat.

"Maybe," Karen replied evenly. "Regardless, as I said, you have to learn to get along with all kinds of people in your life, and you did not make good choices tonight. I think you understand that, don't you, Emily?"

"Yes. That doesn't make it any easier dealing with her and her friends, though."

"Life isn't always easy. You just have to be a better person sometimes. That's not easy to swallow, but later you'll be able to hold your head up high and know you gave the best you had, even when you didn't feel like it."

"Oh, Mother," Emily sighed.

"Emily, I know you don't like it, but that's the way it is. You've got to find a way to work this out, because if you don't, I'm pulling you out of 4-H."

"Mom!" both girls chorused.

"I mean it, Emily Louise," Karen's voice was firm. "You work it out or you won't participate. It's not fair to all the other people who are working hard at this."

"But Mom, it's not fair that I get punished for what Andrea does."

Kim's eyes teared up. This was terrible. What if Andrea wouldn't stop being mean? She just couldn't go to 4-H without her sister being there!

"Emily, you are part of this and that kind of behavior is unacceptable. Do I make myself clear?"

"Yes, Mother."

Emily sighed again and leaned her head in her hand. Her mother was so idealistic about everyone loving each other and getting along.. She just made it sound so easy, and she didn't get how tough it was to be a teenager sometimes.

Kim cried silently all the way home.

That night, after the girls were in bed, Kim's eyes still red and Emily having gone to her room without a word, Karen sat in the darkened living room, thinking.

"Honey, what are you doing?" Jim, wearing cotton pajamas, came out holding his toothbrush in one hand.

"I'm thinking. Something happened tonight and I'm trying to figure out what to do about it."

"Well, come get ready for bed and tell me about it in here— we'll figure it out together."

Karen heaved herself up out of the chair, feeling every bit the forty-year-old woman she was, and followed her slightly balding husband down the hall. He had been holed up in his study when they got home. She knew he was preparing for a big federal trial at the end of the week, so Karen hadn't interrupted him.

Once in bed with alarms set and the lights off, Karen told her husband what had transpired at work night. Jim was appalled.

"I just can't believe Emily would do something like that. She's such a smart girl and she seems to get along with everyone! Either this Andrea is really a piece of work or I don't know Emily as well as I thought," Jim sat up in bed, sounding distressed. "Have I met this Andrea girl?" Jim asked. He didn't attend as many of the work nights and 4-H meetings as Karen did.

"You might have. And you should see her mother—have you met Mrs. Norton?"

"I'm not sure."

"She's the flamboyant, overdressed, glamour type. Blond, big chest, smokes but thinks she hides it."

"Oh yeah, I know the one. No wonder her daughter's a pill," Jim remarked, having dismissed the idea that Emily had turned into some alien he didn't recognize. No way—she'd always been a pretty good kid.

"Well, the bottom line is, these girls have got to learn to get along," Karen told Jim briskly. "I'm just not sure what to suggest. Obviously, we can't trust them to work it out. Apparently, they were body slamming each other like a couple of WWF wrestlers. Oh my God, I can't believe I just said that about my own daughter." Karen put her hands over her eyes in the dark, squeezing her temples.

Next to her, Jim had lain back down and was laughing.

"It's not funny, I know, but it is. We'll think of something. Get some sleep, honey." He leaned over, kissed his wife, and was snoring within five minutes. Karen sighed, lying in the dark, her eyes wide open.

~ FOUR ~

Karen Has a Pop-Up Idea

Very early the next morning, Karen stood leaning against the fence of the paddock, still dressed in her white cotton nightgown with lace around its edges, her feet thrust into worn pink slippers, and a yellow cardigan sweater tossed over her shoulders against the chill. Although the sun was emerging, the morning air was nice, crisp and cool, and smelled of hay, a comforting scent to Karen. She had not slept well. The events of the previous evening had really upset her and she felt she had to come up with some kind of solution.

Prinsessa stood a couple of feet away, her large soft eyes staring right into Karen's. She almost felt as if the little mare were reading her mind. Karen smiled at that thought, amused. She knew that normally you weren't supposed to ever stare directly into horses' eyes because that made them feel dominated, but here again the Icelandics were different. Prinsessa's stare was unwavering and as

43

Karen looked back, a feeling of calm washed over her.

Suddenly, an idea appeared in her head like a pop-up window on a Web page. Karen had no idea what had triggered it, but she realized how brilliant it was. A moment after the idea had struck her, Prinsessa gave a little shake of her head with a small, satisfied whinny and then turned and walked back to the round bale, flicking her tail. Karen stared after her in fascination. It almost felt as if the little mare had inserted the idea into her brain through telepathy. That was outrageous, of course, and she scolded herself for even thinking the thought.

She went back in the house and showered and dressed for the day, but before she started breakfast, she was drawn back outside to spend a few more minutes at the paddock. She'd been out for less than a minute when she turned to see Emily and Kim coming out to feed the horses. Both girls were dressed in khakis, t-shirts with a glittery pattern, and clogs. Kim always sneaked a look at the clothes Emily put out the night before and often copied her style of dress. Since they went to different schools, Emily tolerated it, knowing her little sister looked up to her. Today, Emily had brushed her red-gold hair out and caught it back with a black headband. It was shiny and healthy looking under the bright sun. Kim's darker blond hair was in a high ponytail, clipped with a filigreed gold barrette.

"Whatcha doin', Mom?" Kim called out as they approached, half-tripping in her clogs. Karen grinned to herself; her younger daughter was at that awkward gawky stage that she found endearing. Emily, still reeling from the severe lecture of the previous evening, didn't say anything to her mother, her eyes downcast and her whole body drooping as she followed a few feet behind Kim.

Karen spoke with a touch of excitement, buoyed by her sudden revelation. "I have just had the greatest idea!"

Emily, who had made a beeline straight for the feed cart, looked up, hearing the enthusiasm in her mother's voice. Kim, holding a bucket, replied eagerly, "What, Mommy?"

Karen smiled at the childish reply. "We're going to arrange an overnight trail ride in the Allegheny National Forest! We can coordinate the ride with the Park Rangers so you can stay overnight at the campground in the center of the forest. The rangers staff the campsite all the time and I'm pretty sure they're prepared for groups of young riders coming in and staying overnight if we arrange it ahead of time. Doesn't that sound like fun?"

"Yes!" Kim exclaimed, spilling a little bit of the feed.

"Hold the bucket up, doofus. You're spilling it all over your shoes," Emily told her sister, then asked, "but what do you mean, 'young riders'? Aren't you and Dad coming?" Her hands stilled on the feed cart, watching her mother carefully.

"No," Karen responded, "this would be a ride of friends and foes: you girls and Andrea and maybe a couple others."

"What?!" Emily exclaimed, incredulous. "Are you kidding? Do you really think Andrea and her friends would want to ride with us or that we'd want to go with them? In case you hadn't noticed, we don't like each other."

"This is not about you and them," Karen answered in what Emily considered her mother's "reasonable" tone. "It is about the horses."

"What are you talking about, Mother?" Emily was bewildered, and Kim's head snapped back and forth from her sister to her mother. Her ponytail whipped over to one side, then back, then over, then back—she looked like a horse swishing flies.

"You will invite everyone to ride one of our horses!" Karen told Emily animatedly, as if it were the greatest idea ever, Emily thought. "It would be an all-Icelandic horse trail ride!"

"But Mom…" was all Emily was able to sputter before Karen interrupted.

"Look, I have been up most of the night trying to think of a way to establish some sort of peace between you and Andrea— and these other girls too. Andrea and her mother have a totally different mindset than we do, and we need to show them our point of view. The problem here is a misunderstanding of the Iceys and the best way to help them to understand these horses better, is for those girls to spend some time riding them," Karen finished, in a triumphant tone that suggested it was that simple.

Emily was silent, thinking of the best way to convince her mother that this was such a stupid idea and that there was no way she was going on an overnight trip with Andrea. But, she thought to herself, I have to phrase it in a way that Mom will understand how completely ridiculous it would be.

In those few quiet moments, Kim, who was waiting to see how this was all going to turn out, could hear nothing but the horses munching hay, a big fat bumblebee buzzing in the hollyhocks by the fence, and the hum of a small plane in the distance.

"Mother, it's a complete waste of time anyway, because Andrea would never accept an invitation from me for anything, especially after last night," Emily reasoned. Behind her, Prinsessa had looked up and was watching, almost as if she were following their conversation. The other horses shuffled and snuffled around.

"You don't have to discuss it with her. All you have to do is invite your friends. I'll call Andrea and the other girls' parents and maybe work with the 4-H advisors to get their support. This idea just came to me out of the blue, and girls, you both know what effect these horses have on their riders! Emily, don't you want to resolve this problem and get along with these girls? After all, you do spend a lot of time with them in 4-H and Equestrian Youth Group," Karen told her daughter impatiently.

"Well, I guess..." Emily replied reluctantly, although clearly she wanted to say, "No, not really, not even close!" but didn't want to upset her mother further.

"You'll be glad later you did it and while I certainly don't expect you to become best friends—" Emily couldn't help it, she snorted at that—"then maybe this will provide a way that you can all be civil and tolerate each other."

"Okay," Emily agreed, because she realized Andrea would never say yes, so she didn't really have anything to lose. Suddenly, she felt a lot more cheerful.

"Great!" Karen exclaimed with enthusiasm, thrilled at the change in Emily's response. "Now, let's see," she continued briskly, counting on her fingers, "we have Prinsessa, Skessa, Hela, Kedja, Drasill, Gelmir, Fálki, and Aríel, who can all be ridden on the trail. This will be Aríel's first overnight ride, but I have no doubt that she will behave perfectly, just like her mother. That's enough horses for you two, Emily's three friends, Andrea and her two friends."

"What about one of my friends? Can I invite Darcy?" Kim broke in. She wanted to have a friend of her own along with all the older girls. She had dropped the feed bucket and was twisting the end of her ponytail, a bad habit of hers.

"We'll see, Kim. We're limited in the number of horses we have and getting these girls to get along is the main goal. But," she hastened to say, "not everyone might be able to go, so we'll keep it in mind and invite her if we have a horse for her."

"Mother," Emily told her mother, sounding as if she were warning Karen not to get her hopes up, "just remember, you might not be able to pull this off."

"Just you watch me," Karen retorted with determination and Emily gave an inward groan. With her luck, her mother would talk everybody into it. She was, unfortunately in this situation, really good at convincing people of things.

At that moment, both the discussion and peaceful sounds of nature were interrupted by the melodic tune of Karen's cell phone. She whipped it off her belt and answered. "Yes. All right. What are his vitals? Uh huh, okay, I'm on my way." Karen rushed into the house.

"Don't worry, Emily, it'll be okay," Kim's small voice piped up, trying to reassure her sister as the girls turned their attention back to the feed cart.

"I know, squirt. We'll just see what happens, I guess."

Prinsessa turned away.

· · · · · · · · ·

Karen's day at the clinic was completely chaotic and her focus was entirely on her patients: premature bleeding in a pregnancy, a diagnosis of cancer, a car accident victim with minor injuries, a five-year old boy who had crashed on his bike and split his chin open, requiring stitches, an elderly woman who had fallen and fractured her hip. She did take time during her lunch break to log onto the computer and look up the information about the campground and find out about available dates. By the time she was finished, she had about two minutes left to bolt a salad and gulp some bottled water before her next patient arrived. At 4:30, even though she was tired, she stayed at her desk and decided to make the calls to the other parents about the trail ride, rather than go home and worry about the girls hovering around, listening.

She dialed Virginia Norton and sat back, relaxing her feet on the shelf under her desk.

"Hello?" a woman answered, sounding harried. There was loud TV noise in the background.

"Mrs. Norton?"

"Yes, who is this? Are you selling something? I don't want nothin'."

"No, no. Mrs. Norton, this is Dr. Miller—Emily's mother."

"Oh, you," she responded flatly.

"I wondered if we could chat for a few minutes."

"Yeah, I probably got some stuff I could say to you. Just a minute." She dropped the receiver and went and turned down the TV, then yelled, "Andrea! Turn that music DOWN!" She came back, still grumbling. "Geez, that girl's gonna be deaf before she turns sixteen and I am too, 'cause I gotta turn up the danged TV so loud to hear! Anyway, did you call to give me an apology?"

Karen rolled her eyes. "Mrs. Norton," she said managing to sound pleasant, "I did call to talk about last night, and as a fellow parent, I'm sure you would agree with me that we both need to work together to get this issue resolved, don't you think?"

"Well, yes, I suppose so," Virginia reluctantly agreed. She had heard about her daughter's role in the altercation and realized that Andrea was not blameless. She had seen her in action and also knew that Andrea could be quite difficult at times. Sometimes her throat hurt from screaming at her. She was sure that was the reason and not the few cigarettes she indulged in. Besides, Dr. Miller was a well-known physician in town and maybe if they became friends, she'd get a discount or something. And besides that, it wouldn't do any good to be threatening to sue her like she had last night; her husband was some big shot lawyer. The Norton's money came from her grandmother, an old hag she couldn't stand except for the millions she'd left her when she finally kicked the bucket.

"Good! I knew we'd see eye to eye on this," Karen told her, ecstatic that it was this easy. "Now, I'm realistic and realize that the girls have—uh different personalities..." she said carefully, "...and while I don't expect them to become bosom buddies, I was thinking an overnight trail ride would kind of give them a common bond and an adventure together. We could have their other friends come along and they'd probably really enjoy it, don't you think?"

Karen continued to fill her in on the details of her scheme, the dates that were open, and the cost for the campground. She waved to her receptionist, who had finished confirming next-day appointments and was about to leave. The hallway dimmed as she flipped off the light switch on her way out.

"And since the biggest issue between the girls seems to be the horses themselves, I was thinking that they could all ride Icelandic horses together and get a better understanding of the breed."

"What?!" Mrs. Norton broke in, sounding surprised. "You want everybody to ride your little ponies?" Amused, she said, "Well, sure, why not? If they survive this one together, maybe they can do another ride on real horses and everybody'll be educated."

Dr. Miller bit her tongue and then said as nicely as she could, "Yes, maybe. Do you want to discuss this with your husband and call me back?"

"Oh, no, he's not here. He's gone a lot—I think he's in Florida this week. He trusts me to take care of things here."

"Can I have some cookies? Can I? Can I, Ma, can I?" a little boy's voice reached Karen through the phone.

"No! Go on, git!"

"C'mon, Ma—I want a cookie! I want a cookie!" he screamed at the top of his lungs.

"Shut up!!" Karen heard Andrea's voice coming from a distance.

"I WAAAAAANNNNNT A COOOOOOKIIIIIEEEE!" he screeched at an ear piercing volume.

"Do NOT throw yourself on the floor, Ethan! No! All right, geez, go get one! Quit bugging me!"

Karen sighed. Oh my God, no wonder her husband was gone a lot.

Turning back to the conversation as if nothing out of the ordinary had occurred, Virginia stated she would call Heather and Erica's parents to discuss it with them, and Karen gave her her own home phone number, so they could call with any questions. She stated she would contact Emily's friends. Mrs. Norton said, "Yeah, whatever."

"What about Andrea?"

"What about Andrea?"

"Will she be...amenable...to this?" Karen asked.

"Will she be what?"

"Will she agree?"

"She will because I'll make her agree. We can't have these knock-down, drag out fights anymore."

Dr. Miller was about to agree, when Virginia added, "Andrea was in the worst mood last night and I just can't stand her when she's like that—she's such a pain! It was horrible around here! My nerves can't take it. I might need some kind of nerve pills or something," she hinted.

Karen ignored that. Her head hurt from how many times she had rolled her eyes during the conversation and refrained from suggesting that the family get counseling immediately.

After they hung up, Karen looked at the clock—was that right? Had she been on the phone with Mrs. Norton for only seven minutes? It seemed like a lot longer. She called the families of Emily's other friends. Luckily, everyone was home starting dinner preparations. She pitched the idea to all three, and each thought it was a good idea. They had been to enough work nights and 4-H meetings that they had seen the animosity between the two groups of girls and everyone wanted it resolved. Laura's mother agreed right away, but Hayley's mother said they'd have to see about the dates they chose, because Hayley's grandparents had invited her to spend a month in Newport, Rhode Island, and they weren't sure when she was going yet. Madison couldn't go, because her family had already planned a camping trip out to the Grand Canyon for two weeks.

She made a couple of quick calls to two of the 4-H advisors she was close to, and got their wholehearted agreement as well. They, out of everyone, were most anxious to get the problem between the two girls taken care of, because they had to put up with all the teenage drama, dirty looks, and snide remarks. Enough was enough.

Feeling happier that she had put things in motion and gotten a positive response, Dr. Miller jumped out of her office chair with more energy than she had when she sat down. She decided to stop for the girls' favorite pizza on the way home. That would be a surprise they'd enjoy, unlike the trail ride, which Karen knew Emily did not want to go on at all. Well, they'd go and it'd be fine— Karen knew teenagers thought they already knew everything, but sometimes had to experience life to really figure it out.

She almost skipped on the way to her Lexus SUV, then giggled and looked around to see if anybody had seen. Emily and Kim would just die of embarrassment to see their mother doing that.

The late afternoon sun was warm on her forearm as she unlocked the car and slid into the seat with proper motherly decorum.

~ FIVE ~

The Preparations Begin

Emily stared in disbelief at the hustle and bustle of packing activities going on around her. She just could not believe her mother had pulled this off. School was over and a week had gone by since the uproar at work night. The trail ride was scheduled for the next day. Everyone had come over to the Miller's farm in the evening to get everything ready to go. The men were leaning against the fence rail, talking baseball season and basketball draft choices, with Laura's father, Bruce, and Jim Miller having a healthy argument about the Phillies' chances, and who was going to get drafted first in basketball, and Darcy's dad, Paul, a science professor, giving his analytical assessment of both. Andrea's father was not there; he was still traveling somewhere.

The women were going over details of the trip, the list of supplies—did they have this? Had they thought of that? Andrea's mother, Virginia, was fawning over Karen, telling her, "Great thinking! You're so smart!" whenever Karen suggested something. Laura's mother, Janice, was as outspoken and confident as her daughter, with the same tall, Nordic-blond beauty. She ignored Virginia's gushing and added her own suggestions. Darcy's mother, Annie, was a small, mousy, quiet woman who had tortoise shell glasses and the same shoulder-length brown hair as her daughter. She just nodded and smiled a lot, agreeing with everything. She taught English Literature at the local college and always looked frightened when she was close to the horses. She had such a small frame that she looked as if one swish of a horse's tail could knock her over.

Meanwhile, Laura, Kim, and little Darcy were helping Emily load the trucks with all their tack and saddle packs of clothes, personal items, and some supplies. Andrea stood watching as the others worked. She was dressed to the nines in designer jeans and a silk T-shirt, both of which shouted "new" and "expensive". Her hair was professionally styled specifically for the trip and her makeup had been applied with a heavy hand. Her five-year-old little brother, Ethan, the one who had screamed for a cookie while Virginia was talking to Karen on the phone, was also there. He was amusing himself by chasing grasshoppers, running after them, yelling, and then flinging himself down in the middle of the yard, dizzy and breathing hard. His cowlick was sticking straight up and his jeans were impossibly grass stained.

Emily was actually pretty astonished Andrea was even here,

since her two cohorts weren't able to go. Heather had a babysitting job she'd already committed to for most of the summer, and Erica was taking care of horses, goats, and dogs at her neighbor's farm while they were out of town. They both whined, but their parents made them honor their commitments. Emily figured Mrs. Norton was forcing this on Andrea, the same way her own mother was forcing the trip on her. Thinking about that, she glanced at Andrea with sympathy, then got a hold of herself and shook off that thought.

As for Emily's friends, Hayley had already left for her month in Newport the day before (her grandfather had hollered over the phone, "What are we waitin' for? We're not getting any younger, you know! Put my granddaughter on a plane!") and Madison and her family had left earlier the same day for their Grand Canyon trip. At least her closest friend Laura was going, especially since she was the most confident of the group and had a better chance of holding her own against Andrea.

Since not everyone could go, there were extra horses available, and therefore Kim was allowed to invite Darcy, who was thrilled to be going with the older girls and her best friend. An only child of two absent-minded bespectacled professors, she spent a lot of time at the Millers.

This was going to be an incredible trip and Emily could not wait for it to be over—five girls on five Icelandic horses with no parents on an overnight trail ride! That part was kind of cool. Of course, there would be park rangers at the campsite, but there would also be bunkhouses with comfortable beds and a kitchen with good food. How bad could it be?

Just then, Emily looked over at Andrea, who was holding a small compact mirror and peering at her reflection closely, and gave a little moan. Bad. Very bad.

Emily and Kim had gone on this trail ride with their parents a few times in the last few years and also with the Equestrian Youth Group, but there had always been adults along. This is the first trip where they would be on their own, and not with the best company. She did have to admit that although Andrea had her usual superior attitude, at least she had been a little more cordial since the arrangements for the trail ride had been made. However, Emily had a feeling things would change when they got on the trail and Andrea would show her true colors. Another thing that surprised Emily was that Andrea seemed to be enthusiastic about riding one of the horses. For all the trouble Andrea had given them, Emily guessed envy might have played a major role. Not that she would ever admit that her mother had been right about that.

Laura and Darcy were excited about the trip. They had ridden the Iceys with Emily and Kim before and had always really enjoyed it. Emily had wanted to pick who would ride which horse, but her mother had been adamant about making the selections herself and also had communicated that to everyone involved. Of course,

Emily and Kim would ride their own horses, Skessa and Prinsessa. Karen assigned Andrea to ride Kedja. Since Kedja was a champion show horse, it made sense that Andrea should ride her as she was an accomplished rider. Emily knew Andrea had been riding and showing a good deal longer than she had. Karen wanted Andrea to have a really good ride and maybe Kedja was just the horse to change her attitude about the Icelandics.

Karen was going to put Darcy on Hela. This was a good choice since Darcy was small and wouldn't look out of place on little Hela, but more importantly, Darcy had ridden Hela several times before and knew some of the sly tricks she tried to pull. Laura got Aríel. Again, Emily had to admit this was a good choice. Aríel was the first of the horses born on the Miller farm to reach adulthood and receive her training. She was an excellent horse, just like her mother, Prinsessa. She was young, but Laura was a very good rider who had spent last summer learning to train young horses. Even though each Icelandic horse was unique, they were all safe and easy to ride with wonderful gaits and great personalities. Of course, they were short compared to the horses the other girls were used to. Emily hoped this whole thing would go better than she was expecting, and that both the riders and horses would have good experiences. It still didn't seem like a great idea to her.

Kim slid up alongside of Emily and looked at her troubled expression. "What's wrong?" she asked, unaware of her sister's feelings.

Emily glanced at her little sister, who was still naïve enough to believe that if there were a problem and her mother promised to make it better, it would happen. She wasn't worried at all. She hated to burst Kim's bubble, so she replied, "Uh, um, oh, nothing, I guess."

"I think you just can't believe Mom could arrange all this. This is going to be so cool!" Kim beamed, her shirt half untucked from her hay-flecked faded jeans and some muck on her shoe.

"Yeah, I guess so," Emily replied without a lot of enthusiasm.

Kim opened her mouth to say something else to her sister, but at that moment, the other girls came over to where the two were standing.

"I guess that's it," Andrea said, looking at Emily. "Everything's loaded except the horses."

No thanks to you, Emily thought, but resisted the urge to say it out loud.

"Okay girls," Karen said cheerfully, coming over with the other mothers. "All of you better get home to bed. We need to make an early start to get you on the trail so you can be at camp before dark." Karen looked around at the group, including all the parents.

"We'll meet here about 5:30 tomorrow morning."

Andrea groaned and the other girls looked pained.

Karen ignored their reactions. "We'll load up the horses and be out of here by 6:00. I'll have doughnuts, bagels, and coffee for everyone when you get here. We should be at the park by 9:00 a.m.

and you girls can be on the trail no later than 9:30. It doesn't get dark until 9:00 p.m. now, so you'll have more than enough time to make it to the camp while it's still light. Sound good?"

Everyone nodded in agreement and after a few more suggestions had been made, Laura, Darcy, and Andrea left with their families and headed home. The two truck and trailer combos (one of which had been brought by Laura's parents to transport some of the horses) were parked together in the dark, ready for the morning trip. Not everyone would fit, so Darcy's parents were going to drive their Volvo and take a couple of passengers.

After everyone was gone, Emily sat brooding at the kitchen table while Kim chattered away over cookies and milk. Karen moved around the kitchen, her glasses shoved on top of her head as usual, getting things ready for the early morning snack she had promised everyone. Jim had gone to the den to check his e-mail. He was expecting documentation from one of his colleagues for a legal case he was working on.

After a while Karen became aware of Emily's silence and sat down next to her.

"What's the matter, dear?" her mother asked in a way that made Emily sure she knew exactly what was bothering her. She didn't feel like getting a lecture, so she replied with the usual teenage response, "Nothing, Mom."

"Emily," Karen told her oldest daughter, speaking in her brisk, matter-of-fact way, "I really believe this trip is going to bring peace between you and Andrea. I was watching Andrea tonight when they first got here and she was really getting into the horses. She didn't make any sarcastic comments or even act as if she were being forced to go."

"She just stood around and didn't do anything to help us get loaded," Emily complained.

"You can't expect a miracle. You just have to be glad for the fact that she seems to be enjoying the horses at all, after the way she's behaved. Now, as I said, I believe this little adventure will improve things, but you have to believe it too, and do your part to make it happen."

"I'll help too, Mom," Kim said earnestly, spraying a few cookie crumbs as she spoke.

"I know you will, dear," Karen smoothed Kim's blond ponytail and refrained from admonishing her younger daughter from talking with her mouth full.

"All right," Emily sighed, "but...."

"But what?" Karen asked.

"I have a feeling that things are going to change once we get on the trail with no adults."

"Oh, fiddlesticks," Karen said, using a word she knew made the girls smile, "you know what effect they have on people. These horses—it's impossible to explain—they are magical. You can feel it in their manes; you can see the fire in their eyes. No one can resist them, not even Andrea's group. Let's just give it a try.

"Last summer when you were at 4-H camp, the Stearnses called and asked us to bring a couple horses to the rehearsal dinner for their daughter's wedding. They wanted to have a western theme because the new groom's father had horses out in Denver. I warned Mr. and Mrs. Stearns that he would probably turn up his nose at the Icelandics, but they pleaded and pleaded until I gave in. Alice told me that all they wanted was to take some pre-wedding pictures with the horses. When we got there, the new father-in-law was absolutely infatuated with Prinsessa and Skessa and asked if he could ride them. By the time the evening was over, the horses had given rides to eighty people at the party! Everyone, and I mean everyone, fell in love with them!"

"You never told us any of that, just that you had gone over there with a couple of horses for a party," Kim said, taking a gulp of milk that left a little white rim on her lip.

"That was different," Emily replied, trying to find a way out of the lecture. "Those were adults. Kids are a lot meaner to each other."

Karen thought for a minute, taking her glasses off her head and tapping them on the table. Finally, she said, "You know something? You are going to think I'm crazy, but honestly, I think it was Prinsessa who gave me the idea and... "

Kim interrupted, "What do you mean?"

"Well, don't tell your father; he'll think I'm losing my mind— but what I mean is that I think somehow Prinsessa knew what

I was thinking and she came up with the idea and popped it into my head."

Emily gave her a very skeptical look, but did not argue the point.

"When did this happen?" she asked, her cookies and milk still in front of her, untouched.

"Remember the morning after work night? I was so upset. I hadn't slept very well that night," Karen told Emily, looking at her intently. "I got out of bed as soon as it was light. I went out to the paddock in my pajamas..."

"Mommy!" Kim squealed, thinking of her mother outside in nothing but her nightclothes.

"...and just stood at the fence looking at the horses. That always makes me feel better. Anyway, while I was standing there, Prinsessa walked right up to the fence and looked me right in the eye. I couldn't look away; those big soft eyes are just so deep and full of intelligence."

Unconsciously, Emily nodded in agreement, listening to her mother.

"We were just staring at each other and then after a minute or so, the idea just popped into my head, bing! As soon as I had a clear picture of the trail ride idea with you and Andrea and whoever else could go, Prinsessa gave a little toss of her head and walked back to the round bale. After I had gone in and gotten dressed I just had to come back out again. I had this very odd feeling. I can't really explain it. That was when you two came out to feed the horses. It was just too strange. Six years ago, I would have thought I was imagining it, but after getting to know these horses so well the last few years, I'm not so sure."

The two girls thought about this for a moment, not sure how to respond. Then Kim just had to throw in, "Well, Prinsessa is the smartest horse in the herd. She gets it from me," she added, sounding smug.

They all laughed and Karen saw a distinct change in Emily's expression. She knew that the girls loved the horses very much and believed them capable of anything. Emily appeared to believe the story and Karen felt better.

"Okay, you two, off to bed. We have an early start in the morning." They were shoving the ladder-back chairs away from the table when Jim came in, holding his reading glasses.

"Any cookies left?"

Emily shoved her plate at him. "You're in luck, Dad." She kissed him on the way back to her room. Kim followed closely, but she flung herself at their father, almost knocking the reading glasses out of his hand as she gave him a big hug.

Karen sat back down at the table with her husband as he ate Emily's snack and they finished the evening talking in murmured tones.

~ SIX ~

A Trail with No End

The next morning the entire group stood munching doughnuts and bagels slathered with cream cheese while they watched the sun rise over the beautiful green hills. The birds chirped cheerfully; everyone snuggled into their fleece jackets and sweatshirts against the nip of the air. The parents sipped coffee and waited for the caffeine to kick in, while the girls drank orange juice out of paper cups. The horses were loaded, with the ones staying behind staring at the trailers with such focus that they looked as if they were saying goodbye. Of course, everyone had a good-natured laugh at Prinsessa's loading technique—first the little hop with her front legs, then the little hop of the back ones, but it was all in good fun and Kim felt so excited that, for once, it didn't bother her.

After finishing their early breakfast, everyone settled into the cars and the caravan departed for Allegheny National Forest.

Andrea's mother, Virginia, had just dropped her daughter off, having left her little boy at home by himself, still sleeping. The other parents clucked their disapproval when she announced that. She ruffled Andrea's hair (much to Andrea's annoyance), said, "Have fun on the pony ride!" got back in her car and drove off, immediately lighting up a cigarette. A tiny trail of smoke came out of the car window as she zoomed off down the road. Andrea stared after her and sighed, then climbed into the backseat of one of the trucks and slunk down, staring out the window and refusing to say anything, although her eyes were wide open.

The group traveled to the Pennsylvania Turnpike Northeast Extension and then headed east on I-80. It was a three-hour drive and everyone was so excited that it seemed like it took forever, but actually, they made it to the trailhead right on time. Arriving so early, they were the only ones in the parking lot, and there was a cool, grassy, shady area right next to it with plenty of room to spread out and get organized. Even Andrea got into the spirit of the thing; she jumped out of the truck and started grabbing tack and equipment.

"Andrea! Come help me get Kedja unloaded," Kim called, and Andrea dropped her armful and went right over. Emily watched for a few seconds, surprised. Kim chattered away as she and Andrea unloaded Kedja and Skessa. Andrea, not finding Kim a threat, listened and even put in a word here and there. Emily even noticed a couple of genuine smiles cross Andrea's face, and realized the girl actually looked prettier without all the makeup she usually wore.

"You're so lucky to be riding Kedja—she's such a great horse. Well, you'll find out, you're just going to love her!" Kim enthused. Andrea, without her mother standing there, felt free enough to step up to Kedja and stroke her nose and her neck. Funny little horse, you seem okay, she thought to herself. Kedja eyed Andrea with curiosity and submitted to her strokes, closing her eyes briefly.

When all the horses were unloaded, the girls began to tack up while the parents went to the park office to register and check in the riders. The forms and information took a while, so by the time they came back out, the girls were mounted and walking the horses around the field next to the trailhead. Kim and Darcy rode together, leaning toward each other and giggling.

Laura sat tall in Aríel's saddle, back straight, her long blond braid a thick rope hanging down her back, her finely chiseled cheekbones pink. She held the reins with ease as she rode over to Emily, smiling. Andrea, wearing fancy riding pants and a lacy T-shirt, rode Kedja with technical skill, but didn't look entirely comfortable on the unfamiliar horse.

Karen called them over, handed out park instructions and then distributed three trail maps, one to Emily, one to Andrea, and one to Laura. The girls folded them and stuck them in an outside pocket of their saddlebags.

"Okay, now, hop down and listen up," Karen said authoritatively to the group, who gathered around her in a half circle. They all dismounted and held their reins, the horses a few feet behind them. "All of you have done this ride before with either family or the Equestrian Youth Group and you know the trails are clearly marked. I don't want you drifting off the main trail. It will take between seven and eight hours to reach the camp-site so you have plenty of time to take breaks and each of you has a snack in your pack and lunch for today and plenty of water. The rangers will have dinner for you tonight and both breakfast and a box lunch tomorrow for your ride back. Everything is paid for, so you don't need any money. There's pretty good cell service along the whole trail, and if you have any problems, call the park office first—the number's on the paper I just gave you..." Karen interrupted herself as she saw Kim's mouth open to ask the question "...then one of us. Any questions? Wait! You remembered your cell phones, right?"

Andrea, Emily, and Laura nodded. It had been decided that three would be plenty and the younger girls didn't need to take one.

Karen thought the girls looked like Kentucky Derby riders ready to explode out of the starting gate. Nobody had any more questions.

"Well, okay, then," Karen finished, "we'll be here with the trailers by 6:00 p.m. tomorrow, so no lollygagging around on your way back." Darcy and Kim giggled at this, and Andrea rolled her eyes. Who said that kind of thing, anyway? "We don't want to have to be sitting here waiting for you. Give a call when you think you're about a few hours away so we can be here at the same time, but if we don't hear from you we'll be here by 6:00. Now say goodbye to your folks."

Laura's parents enveloped her in big smothering hugs; Darcy's professor parents patted her shoulders nervously and gave her a light kiss on the cheek; Kim again threw herself at her father for a bear hug and kissed her mother; Emily hugged her father in more reserved fashion and gave her mother a hug too. As her mother hugged her, she whispered to Emily, "Now, you and Laura include Andrea too—remember why you're doing this."

"I will, Mom. Don't worry," Emily told her, hugging her again.

Andrea stood to the side. Karen couldn't help herself—she stepped over to her and hugged her too.

"I'll be your mother for a minute today," she said, her tone light and casual. Andrea, was stiff and unyielding under Karen's unexpected touch, but Emily noticed the other girl's eyes were filled with tears.

"Thanks," Andrea said gruffly. She awkwardly patted Karen's back and stepped away.

The girls mounted up and turned their horses around, the parents all waving and calling, "Have fun! See you tomorrow! Love you! Be careful!"

"We will! Don't worry! Love you too! See you later!" the girls called back.

They headed up the wooded hill to the trailhead, hyped up and breaking into a canter, but when they reached the trail, the Icelandics automatically fell into single file according to their own pecking order. Unbeknownst to most people, Iceland has a surprisingly large amount of quicksand in many areas. That, combined with the rocky, craggy landscape, had taught the Icelandics to select a lead horse and follow in that horse's footsteps. The lead horse was on the lookout for quicksand and picked out the best path, while the rest stayed in line behind it. This was obviously not necessary on an American park trail, but it was so ingrained into the Icelandics' natural instincts that they automatically started out this way.

Icelandic horses have great temperaments, but it was still important for Andrea, Laura, and Darcy to learn to ride their new horses properly. Although Icelandic horses belong to a unique breed, they are still horses, and each girl needed to develop a strong relationship with the horse she was riding. Balance, cuing, and awareness of the horse's personality were critical components so they could all enjoy a good trail ride on their new horses.

Andrea found she was having a completely different riding experience on Kedja than she had ever had on her highly strung thoroughbred, Star.

Kedja walked with her head held high in a regal manner. She was a bay mare, almost black. Her extraordinary mane, forelock and tail were very long and thick—a classic Icelandic look.

It did not take Andrea long to realize that in some ways Kedja was a lot like the highly trained show horses she had ridden in the past, as far as her sensitivity to cues and responding well to them. However, Andrea quickly learned that in other ways, Kedja was different from any other horse she had ridden. She had always used very severe bits and crops to cue Star. Kedja was the most sensitive and responsive horse she had ever ridden, and right away Andrea picked up Kedja's preference that she not keep any pressure on the reins. She preferred to have the reins loose at all times and only a tiny touch to the right or left would get her to turn. Leg cues were the same. Andrea did not need a spur of any sort with Kedja. A tiny bit of leg pressure could get her to move ahead, sideways, or any other dressage move, incredibly beneficial on the trail.

Andrea also had to learn to adjust to Kedja's gaits. As a five-gaited horse, she could walk, tölt (a smooth gait, slower than a trot but faster then a walk), trot, canter, and pace. Getting her to switch between gaits was a lot like shifting gears in a car. Just a tiny bit of leg pressure would pop her up a gait. Andrea had a light touch and felt that Kedja and she were quickly in tune with each other. Andrea's unsettled and chaotic home life caused her to pour out affection with horses and this was no different. It did not take Andrea long to fall in love with Kedja, although she hid her feelings from the other girls.

Darcy had ridden Hela before but not on a long trail ride. Hela, an easy horse to ride, was very intelligent and even though she was under thirteen hands, seventeen years old, and had had many babies, she took to the trail like the Energizer Bunny. Her hooves were tough as iron, and she was not afraid of anything or even interested in anything but grass. This was her only bad habit. If her rider were not paying attention and she saw a nice patch of grass on the side of the trail—that was it. In a second, she had her head down, grabbing as much grass as she could before her rider could pull her back onto the trail. Like Kedja, Hela did not need aggressive bits and spurs. She would give in after a little fight to get the grass, but on the trail her rider could drop the reins and she would plug along without any guidance. She didn't care if she was in front or back or even by herself. Except for her little grub grabbing tricks, she was a great horse and Darcy and she were very compatible together. Darcy was an easygoing rider who enjoyed the quiet company of her horse—she admired the scenery, gabbed with Kim, and daydreamed by herself, moving comfortably in tandem with Hela and not demanding anything of her. Hela allowed her to do all those things. Hela had always been the low horse on the totem pole, but she was very smart and often performed little actions to show she was not as low as the others thought her. Hela looked like a flea-bitten gray in the summer, but when she got her winter coat she looked like a great white powdered doughnut.

Laura and Aríel made a perfect match—beautiful, outgoing, confident, and possessing a strong character. Aríel was a blend of her parents, Prinsessa and Hersir. A bay like her mother, Aríel had a huge forelock, mane, and tail, and a strong Alpha personality. She had only started her training last spring, quickly learning her cues. Her gaits were natural and she was learning to have respect for her riders. Aríel also had the strength of her father, more energy than a race car, and a very inquisitive nature. Anything she saw that she had not seen before or didn't understand, she wanted to investigate immediately. She preferred to go fast, but could walk slowly and stay with the other horses if that was the pace that was set. She was large for her age. At almost fourteen hands, she had the huge powerful neck of her father. Laura loved all of these traits. She had worked with young horses before and loved their spunk and enthusiasm. She liked to ride them hard, but worked to keep them in line. Aríel loved everybody and instantly bonded with Laura. Laura felt a kinship with Aríel, recognizing the same spirit and appreciation for life. A good-natured teenager, Laura exuded confidence and the willingness to try new things. She liked almost everybody she met, and was able to find something interesting about everyone.

Prinsessa and Skessa belonged to Kim and Emily, devoted and fiercely loyal to their horses. Prinsessa was very short, maybe a touch more than twelve hands. At eighteen years of age, she had borne twelve babies, but it hadn't affected her energy level. Like Aríel and Kedja, she had a thick mane and forelock, and a tail so long it dragged on the ground behind her. Prinsessa was the boss of the whole herd, the Alpha mare, and there was never any question of it with the other horses. Gentle enough for anyone, even a small child, to ride, her gaits were smooth, and she could tölt for hours on end. In spite of her small size, she had no problem carrying an adult on the trail. Kim loved Prinsessa wholeheartedly and was very affectionate to her. Prinsessa seemed to return Kim's passion and the two were inseparable.

Skessa, a chestnut, was totally different. She had had five babies, was a little younger than Prinsessa, but she was almost fourteen hands, large for an Icelandic. Skessa had a broad chest and back and was enormously powerful. A rare six-gaited horse, she could do the "flying pace" at speeds of up to thirty-two mph. Her great power made her perfect for jumping and, regardless of her size and girth, she could show in dressage with such grace that the judges were often amazed. Skessa and Prinsessa were close and liked to ride together. Emily loved Skessa with a passion; the two had formed an immediate and lasting bond. When Emily came out to the barn, Skessa was always right next to her, Emily's affectionate hand resting on her.

Once the girls had entered the trail, they were able to urge the horses and stayed grouped together. Kim and Darcy rode side by side, both gabbing, sometimes at the same time.

Laura and Emily caught up to each other and started talking, but Emily remembered her mother's words and said, "C'mon, Andrea, come up closer to us so you can hear!"

Andrea replied, "I'm still getting used to Kedja. I'll just ride back here for a little bit."

Laura and Emily looked at each other.

"No, I'm fine, really," Andrea said a little testily, then softened a bit. "Kedja is very sensitive and I'm used to using an aggressive bit and spurs. When I can loosen up and cue her like she's used to, I'll come up."

"Okay."

Laura and Emily proceeded to chatter about various things, the dismal reality shows on TV so far that summer, the vacation Laura's family was taking in August to California, the new flavors of ice cream they had at the health food store, which sounded disgusting ("Who wants wheat germ or liquefied spinach in ice cream? Blech!"). Laura made a horrible face and they both burst into laughter, feeling young and carefree out on their own on this adventure.

Andrea could overhear them and they seemed so easy and comfortable with each other. Her friendships with Heather and Erica weren't like that. They were always talking about shopping, competing to have the most expensive thing bought that week, or complaining about their parents. Andrea realized they didn't ever really listen to each other; they were too busy talking about themselves. But it was different with Emily and Laura—they seemed more like sisters, able to talk about little things, laughing a lot, having fun together. Andrea felt strange. She didn't know how to have a friendship like that. She frowned.

Kim and Darcy's conversation drifted back to Emily and Laura.

"It is so true—Allen McGuire told Sam that Rob thinks you're cute!"

"No way! He did not say that!" Kim shrieked in response to Darcy's statement.

"Way! He's not as cute as the guy who won the blue ribbon in the New York state news section of 4husa.org, though."

"Oh, I know, I saw that—I was surfing the site yesterday—that guy is so hot!" Kim squealed. "Should I e-mail him?"

"You wouldn't dare!"

Laura and Emily looked at each other and started to laugh. They remembered being twelve and consumed by who was cute and who liked whom and nobody did anything about it, but it was fun to talk about.

The morning was absolutely beautiful and the horses were comfortable on the trail. The girls soon became so focused on their conversations that they let the horses move along themselves without paying a lot of attention to them. They watched for wildlife, looked at the beautiful scenery and stopped for snacks and lunch.

Andrea did come up and join a little bit into Laura and Emily's conversation, although she was still pretty standoffish. The other two girls were careful not to discuss any of their friends, but to keep the topics neutral. They did talk about their teachers, whom they hoped to get the next year: "Mr. Alexander—he's sooo nice!" "But not Mrs. Hagland! Her name fits her—what a hag—and that wart thing she has on her neck!" "Ewww! Laura! Stop it!" Andrea and Emily cried in stereo, looking at each other and laughing. That seemed to break the ice.

Andrea told Laura and Emily, "Well, Kedja is a really sensitive horse. Boy, you just need to touch her to get a response from canter to stop, pretty different than I expected. Although," she had to add, "my horse, Star, is really an elite specimen, which is why I picked her. I can get pretty much anything I want out of my parents."

Laura and Emily ignored that, knowing Andrea couldn't lose face. But they noticed she spent a lot of time leaning forward patting Kedja on the neck and murmuring to her. Emily turned forward and gave a satisfied smile.

"C'mon, you guys!" Kim hollered from her spot in back after lunch. "Let's tölt!"

"What's that?" Andrea looked horrified.

"The Icelandics are very famous for their smooth gait—it's faster than a lot of horses' trot, but not quite a canter," Emily told her. "But they also do short bursts of cantering and trotting too. Oh, my gosh, sorry, I sounded just like my mother, lecturing like that!"

Andrea smiled. "That's okay—I want to try a smooth tölt! Let's go!"

And they took off.

They were having a great time. About mid to late afternoon, they came to a wide clearing and Laura suggested they stop for one more granola bar, water, and stretch, and bathroom break. Hela had already gotten a head start—as soon as they slowed down, she was munching grass like crazy. After their break, they remounted and headed off on the last leg to the campground. The late afternoon air became warmer and since there was no breeze, it felt stuffy and humid. The girls were tired and their lively chatter had pretty much tapered off to a remark here and there.

"Want another sip of water, Darcy?"

"Oh, no thanks, Kim."

Then they'd subside back into silence. They were so comfortable that they rode along in a kind of a sleepy trance. Once again, the horses dropped back and settled into single file in the order they determined. Prinsessa was first—she was always first—then Skessa, who was like Prinsessa's lieutenant. Next came Kedja, who was also an Alpha mare. After Kedja came Aríel. Bringing up the rear was Hela who was lowest in the herd, but didn't mind and actually enjoyed being last, being able to snatch a few mouthfuls of grass and get away with it. So it was Kim, Emily, Andrea, Laura, and then Darcy. The girls were comfortable enough to let the horses take the lead and let them go, riding along the trail, not paying close attention to their surroundings.

During the sleepy late afternoon, Prinsessa quietly and smoothly left the main path, and forked off on a smaller branch of trail. No one noticed. The path looked well used and the girls were so drowsy that it didn't even occur to them that they weren't on the main path anymore. They followed this trail for almost an hour without a break, everyone either dozing a bit or kind of zoned out.

Suddenly, a breeze of cool air pushed its way through the trees and all the girls came to with a start, sitting up in their saddles at the same time.

"I wonder how far we are from the camp," Andrea remarked, pulling her trail map out of the saddlebag pocket and unfolding it.

"I'm not sure," Emily replied, sounding puzzled, "but I don't see any trail markers. Nothing looks familiar to me. How about anyone else?" she asked, thinking it had been a whole year since she'd been up here, so maybe she just didn't remember.

"Me either, but I'm hungry," Kim yawned and stretched. The other girls chimed in that they were hungry too.

"This trail doesn't look very well used." Emily sounded nervous and Kim gave her a sharp look. The sun was beginning to set behind the trees and it was getting shadowy in the woods.

Kim perked up from her place in the lead and pointed. "Oh, wait! There's the camp up there! Yay, dinner!" There was a bright spot ahead. The trees were so close and the canopy so thick that the bright spot looked like the opening of a tunnel. Together the girls accelerated the horses into a canter and ran for the opening in the woods, calling, "I want s'mores! I want a hamburger!" Within a minute they had exited the woods and cantered headlong into blazing sunlight. Temporarily blinded, they shielded their eyes, drew up together and the horses stopped.

~ SEVEN ~

Where Are We?

O h, Mother, that was wonderful!" said a sweet young feminine voice. "I'm so excited! Oh, how beautiful it is! When will the herd be here? Will Kafteinn be with them? I can't wait to tell Father...."

"Patience, daughter," said an older female voice, sounding deep and wise.

Kim, Emily, Laura, Andrea, and Darcy all each felt as if they were hearing these voices coming from inside their heads. Blinking as their eyes gradually became accustomed to the bright sunlight, they saw before them a long flat plain sloping off into the distance. They could not see the end of it. It looked flat, but there was actually a very subtle slope to it, and it was covered with a short brownish-green grass. Not a shrub, tree, rock, or boulder was to be seen anywhere, but a river ran down the center of the valley. The plain stretched almost five kilometers across and running along its sides disappearing into the distance were huge mountains with snow-covered peaks.

"Wha...wha...what happened?" Andrea stuttered in a shaky voice, looking around in awe.

"I don't know," Emily replied in a hushed tone. "Where are we?"

With these words, everyone suddenly found their voices and began to talk at once in a babble of voices.

"I don't recognize anything."

"What should we do?"

"Somebody get the trail map."

"Hel-lo—this is not on the trail map."

"I'm scared." That was Kim.

"Don't be scared, peanut," Emily told her sister. "Come over here by me."

"Should we just go back the way we came?"

"I don't know."

"Emily, get your cell phone out—let's call Mom."

"Good idea, Kim." Emily reached into her saddlebag and pulled out her phone. The screen was blank. She pushed the "on" button. Nothing.

"It's dead."

"Dead," Laura echoed, peering at her own phone.

"Nothing on mine either," Andrea added.

"Oh no, what are we going to do?"

"I don't know, what we should do!"

"Silence!" commanded the deep woman's voice they had heard a few minutes ago.

"You heard my mother," the other youthful feminine voice piped up. "Shut up!"

"Silence to you as well, daughter."

The girls immediately stopped talking and started looking around for who was speaking, twisting in the saddles, looking this way and that.

"Excuse me," Emily asked politely. "But, where are you?" She felt like Wilbur the pig in *Charlotte's Web*, looking for the spider.

"Below," said the woman's voice.

All the girls looked down at the ground.

"Below where?" Emily could not really believe this was happening. Was she dreaming this?

"Below your sister. She has the honor to be in my saddle and in my care."

"Prinsessa," Kim burst out. "Oh, Prinsessa, you can speak! Prinsessa, Prinsessa!!"

"Easy, child," said Prinsessa, "Hush, now."

"Kim—are you nuts? She can't talk—she's a horse! This is some kind of a trick," Andrea snorted derisively, peering at Kim and Prinsessa. "Did you guys bring me here to set me up for some joke to get even with me? Is that it?" Her voice rose hysterically.

"Silence, silly child," Prinsessa commanded in a booming voice.

Andrea's mouth dropped open in a little o.

All of the girls stared in wonder at Prinsessa. Nothing was moving but her large nostrils as she breathed in and out.

"I, I ...don't understand, uh, Prinsessa," Emily said.

"If you and everyone else will be quiet for a moment, I will explain," replied Prinsessa patiently.

"Yes, ma'am," replied Emily.

"We, the horses of Iceland," began Prinsessa in a lecturing tone, "have evolved over 1,000 years as a single herd. We have survived subfreezing temperatures, the elimination of nearly all our food, horrific volcanic explosions, and many other environmental disasters. As a reward for our survival, the great Icelandic Horse God, Sleipnir, the eight-legged steed of Óðinn, gave us special powers. You may think of it as magic, but they are not unlike human strengths. Some of us are blessed with more than others. The mares of our herd have the greatest of these powers. One of the powers includes the ability to speak with our sires from long ago and to travel to them when we are needed. And, of course, we can speak with our minds. Not to everyone, and not always clearly, but we can always speak with each other."

"But if you can speak to us now," asked Kim, "why couldn't you speak to us at home?"

"We did," Prinsessa told her with a little humor in her voice, "but you humans chose not to listen, or would not have believed we could."

"I would have believed it! And I'm a good listener!" said Kim staunchly, a bit upset.

"Of course," replied Prinsessa. "I always knew what you were thinking. And while we could not speak as clearly as we are now, maybe you had some idea of what I was thinking?"

"Well, yes, I do believe that's true!" Kim nodded so hard, her ponytail bobbed up and down.

"In addition, Kimberly, I have heard you defend me and the other horses many times. You are to be commended for that. Others still have quite a lot of learning to do." Prinsessa gave Andrea a stern look and she had the grace to look sheepish.

"Now, to continue," Prinsessa went on, "our great sire has called us to this time and place to help. We have arrived in northern Iceland near the villages of Hólar and Akureyri. It is about 800 years before you were born."

The mare heard a gasp from the girls and their fear was almost a tangible thing in the air surrounding them. "Do not worry, or be afraid," Prinsessa tried to reassure them. "Each of your horses can speak with you and all of us will care for you."

"Ohhhh...." At this point, Darcy was completely overcome by the whole experience. Shocked by all she was hearing and wondering if she was going crazy, her vision faded, little black spots appeared in front of her, and sounds became faint. Darcy's eyes rolled back in her head, and she passed out and fell off Hela, landing on the ground with a little thump. Kim gasped and leaped off Prinsessa, running through the stubby grass to her friend.

"Darcy! Darcy! Are you all right?" She flung herself down.

"Oh, that's just great," said Hela sarcastically as she put her nose to Darcy's head. "So typical of a human."

"Hela," Kim scolded, "don't be so mean! How do you expect us to feel? This is a little much for us to believe."

Hela softly nudged Kim, apologizing, "Yes, you're right. I'm sorry. Move over a little bit. I can help her."

Kim shifted out of the way, and watched as Hela leaned down and snuffled in Darcy's hair and ear. A few moments later, Darcy's eyes opened and she stared up at Hela, locking gazes with her. Calm seemed to come over Darcy, and Kim watched as she sat up, seeming mentally to shake herself off and said, "Thank you, Hela. I feel much better now."

"You're welcome, dear."

To Kim's surprise, Darcy got to her feet and leaned against Hela's side, looking expectantly at Prinsessa as if nothing were out of the ordinary.

"Go ahead, girls, and make a proper acquaintance with your horses," Prinsessa instructed.

Emily jumped off Skessa and gave her a great big hug. "Oh, Skess, all this time you knew just how I felt and what I was thinking! And I had no idea!"

"Yes, it's true," said Skessa solemnly, "and while I might not always be the best communicator, I feel like we are both bound together by a love that has always warmed my heart. Quite frankly," she continued, "I have always had a hard time with emotion. I am a warrior and we tend to bury our feelings deeply. You are different, young lady—I have cared for you greatly since the first time we rode together."

"Oh, Skessa, I feel the same way!" Emily told her, hugging her neck.

Andrea had dismounted and was eyeing Kedja warily. She stood stiffly and finally said, "How do you do?" and then felt like a complete idiot. What did you say to a talking horse, for goodness sake?

"I understand how you feel, Andrea," Kedja told her in a serious tone. "You are a good girl at heart and an excellent rider. I enjoyed our ride through the woods together today."

"Uh…this is all a little strange for me," Andrea sounded hesitant, but went on, "but I am very happy to meet you and I was impressed with your showmanship skills."

"Yes," said Kedja in her solemn and deep voice, "I know you have always thought us ponies, but I think this journey will teach you much more. In addition, you have other lessons to learn and I think you will gain much knowledge about yourself during this journey."

"I think it is going to take me a while to get used to all of this," said Andrea, half to herself and half to Kedja.

"Don't worry," said Kedja," things will come together sooner than you think."

Laura and Aríel bonded right away. Since technically the two were about the same age in horse and human years, they were like two teenage girls thrown together in a bizarre situation.

"Aríel," Laura excitedly jumped off her saddle, "is this your first trip? Do you have magic too? Are you…."

"Whoa," said Aríel, "slow down, girl. Yes, this is my first 'Journey' and I sure hope I have powers. I haven't had a chance to use them yet, but I'll be damned if I don't get to use them here!"

Prinsessa overheard this and replied with a sharp, "Aríel, watch your mouth!"

Aríel snickered to Laura and they bowed their heads together, giggling.

"I'm glad I got paired up with you, Aríel. Oh my gosh, this is so awesome! I think that the two of us are going to do great things together," Laura told her, feeling empowered.

"How right you are, my dear. How right you are," Prinsessa murmured to herself.

Kim, being Kim with her youthful exuberance and flair for the dramatic, ran over to Prinsessa and flung her arms around her neck. With a special tolerance for her young charge, Prinsessa allowed this and returned the affection, rubbing against Kim's arms.

Prinsessa permitted the girls to get to know their horses for a few minutes. Then she took control again.

"Silence," she commanded.

Prinsessa moved away from the rest of the horses and turned to face them. The other horses stood in a semi-circle around her except for Skessa, who stepped to Prinsessa's right side. The girls had let their reins drop and the horses were setting themselves up without guidance. It was the horses that were in charge now. As soon as Prinsessa had spoken, the group fell silent.

"You will not be afraid anymore because I have used my powers to bestow on you a feeling of security and anticipation."

"Prinsessa, I do feel strange," said Emily, and the other girls nodded. "I feel as if I should be afraid, but I'm not. It's more of a feeling that something exciting is about to happen!"

Andrea, who was about to make fun of Emily for sounding so goofy, opened her mouth, but then she realized she felt the same way. Hmm, that was odd.

At the same time, the girls felt their confusion and memories about the trail ride and home soften and fade into the background. The atmosphere around them became crystal clear and sharp, the sky more intense, the detail of each blade of grass magnified. All the girls felt as if they were clearly present in the here and now and could focus on what was happening and what they were here for, not what they had left behind.

"This is good," replied Prinsessa. "You feel my powers, and soon you will feel more, but do not interrupt. I must speak of serious things."

The girls listened intently as she continued, "There is a great sire here who has called for our help. His name is Kafteinn, which means "Captain." When I learned of the problems here, I realized we would need the help of humans from our time. I thought for many days as to how this task should be accomplished. My chief aide is Skessa. We have often traveled here, as there is much strife among the people of this time."

Skessa bowed her head to the other girls and Emily beamed with pride at her horse.

"It was Skessa," continued Prinsessa, "who came up with the plan. She thought of it on the night after you, my Emily, had foolishly chosen to battle Andrea. I say foolishly, because you are about to see what real anger, hatred, and battle is like."

Emily and Andrea looked at each other feeling guilty. A part of Andrea felt as if there were something unbelievably weird about this, but another part of her felt as if she belonged here with these horses and these girls. It was an odd feeling, because Andrea never felt as though she had ever really belonged anywhere. She looked at Emily again, and the two shared an unspoken agreement that all things would be put behind them for now and they would move forward together.

"After that night," Prinsessa was speaking, "Skessa felt the emotions of Karen. She thought of this trip and told me of her idea. The morning after, I spoke with Karen and gave her the plan for the trail ride. I could not speak to her as we are speaking now, but I was able to give my thoughts to her."

"Mom knew it was you, Prinsessa," interrupted Kim. "She told us she thought you gave her the idea!"

"Your mother, little one, is very intelligent for a human, but you have interrupted your elder," Prinsessa reprimanded her.

"I'm sorry," Kim said, with a twinge of excitement that made it sound like not much of an apology.

"Karen followed through as we had hoped and now we are here. Soon Kafteinn and the herd will come, so I must speak quickly. As I said, I am the leader of this small herd and Skessa is my aide. Each horse and girl has unique and very useful capabilities. Now," Prinsessa continued, "you can see that we are standing at the end of a long river valley. At the other end of this valley is a small farming village where we will be going. It is called Hólar and is populated by kind and gentle people. Hólar is also the home of a great herd of our ancestors. If you look back in the other direction, you can see a fishing village called Akureyri. The chieftain and people of Akureyri are the ones who are fighting with Hólar."

It was at that moment that the girls realized the woods in which they had been traveling were gone. This was a bit of a shock, and without thinking of Prinsessa's need to give them more information, they all ran back a hundred yards to look at where the forest had been. What they found was a steep volcanic rock cliff, which tumbled down to a deep fjord. It was surrounded by the same mountains that followed the plain. The fjord led out to the blue sea, which they could see sparkling in the distance, dotted with little whitecaps. At the bottom of the cliff and on the west side of the fjord, they could see a village with boats, people, and horses. At this moment, Prinsessa and the other horses ran up behind the girls and Prinsessa hissed, "Get down! You must not be seen!"

All the girls dropped to the grass and lay flat on the ground, peering over the cliff. The horses stood back so they were not visible either.

"The weather has deteriorated in the last few years and food has become scarce for both villages. The chieftain of Akureyri, Siklingur, has gathered weapons and men to battle Hólar in order to take their crops and horses. They have come to Hólar several times, but the people of Hólar were prepared and fought them off. Skessa and I have come back to help with two of these battles. Our sires originate from Hólar."

This time Andrea spoke up. "Is there another battle coming? Are we to help fight?" The powers Prinsessa had placed within her were taking effect like a drug.

"Something much worse has happened," continued Prinsessa, restraining the urge to rebuke Andrea for interrupting. "Gígja, the daughter of Arnþor, who is the chieftain of Hólar, loves to ride fast and free over the plain. She has a strong will and spirit, is very beautiful and carries much of her father in her. She is about the same age as you girls, maybe a little older. Siklingur knew she liked to ride out on the plain, and sent spies to hide along the valley and wait for her. A few days ago, they captured her and took her to the dungeons of the Great House at Akureyri. Siklingur has sent messengers to Arnþor telling him that his daughter will be killed if he does not relinquish his rule to Siklingur. Arnþor is so distraught that he has locked himself up in a room and will not speak to anyone. The village is afraid, for they feel that their leader has abandoned them. We are here at the bidding of Kafteinn, leader of the herd at Hólar, to rescue Gígja and return her to her father."

By this time the girls had slid down the slope out of view and were sitting by their horses looking at Prinsessa and Skessa with eagerness. They were eager to enter into this unknown—and possibly exciting— adventure.

Taking the lead, Laura spoke up first. "Prinsessa, how will we be able to help? We don't speak the language here and obviously we don't know anything about being in a war." The other girls nodded in agreement.

Prinsessa was ready to take questions now, and answered kindly, "I have given you the power to speak and understand the language of the people and the horses here. Like the humans of your time, the people of these villages cannot speak directly to the herd, but they have more intuition of our powers than your people and we can often send our thoughts to them."

At that moment, Skessa nudged Prinsessa and said, "I hear the coming of the herd! Should I go to meet them and prepare them for what they will find?"

"No," Prinsessa replied. "Kafteinn already knows I have brought the children and he has prepared the others." She then turned back to the rest of the girls and said, "Ladies, you must stand and bow your heads to Kafteinn when the herd arrives. Speak only when you are spoken to. I will do all the talking. Daughter, come and stand at my left." Aríel moved over immediately and looked expectant.

It was not long before the girls heard a thundering roar coming up the valley. They all jumped to their feet and squinted, but could not see anything but a cloud of dust.

"Hela!" Darcy hissed. "Quit eating and get over here!"

"Mmm—bbb—sorry," Hela said with her mouth full from several feet away where she had found some particularly sweet grass and was eating like there was no tomorrow. She stepped back toward the other horses, still munching, as they began to see the herd galloping toward them. As they had been instructed, they stood and bowed their heads to show submission, although Emily had to elbow Kim, who was still watching the arrivals with fascination.

"Isn't this exciting?" Aríel murmured to Laura, who was leaning against her, one arm on her back.

"Yes!" Laura whispered back.

Within a couple of minutes, the herd roared up to them and came to a stop. At the lead was a beautiful silver dappled stallion, followed by about a hundred horses of many different colors, but all with the familiar look of their own Icelandic horses.

Kim whispered to Emily with her head down, "That must be Kafteinn; he looks just like Hersir."

"Sh-h…" was all she got back.

It was, in fact, Kafteinn, and he marched proudly up to Prinsessa, shaking his mane back regally. Unlike the girls and other horses who all had their heads bowed, Prinsessa held her head high. In spite of the fact that she was a good deal shorter than Kafteinn, Prinsessa stood proud and Kafteinn nodded his head in acknowledgment of her supremacy.

"Welcome, great daughter of the far future. We are thankful that you have come," said Kafteinn in a strong and commanding tone.

"We are of the herd," replied Prinsessa. "We will always come when you call for us."

"I see you have brought the humans of your time," Kafteinn continued, looking around at the group. "This has never happened before, but it will be most helpful." He paused for a second, then looked at Aríel. "Ah, you have brought your daughter. Welcome, Daughter of Prinsessa, to the land of your sires."

Aríel looked up into the eyes of Kafteinn and said crisply, "My name is Aríel." At this, Prinsessa gave her a swift kick with her hind leg and Aríel immediately lowered her head.

Kafteinn laughed. "You have your mother's fiery spirit, Aríel.

This is good, very good. And you are tall and strong. I think you will have great powers and be a grand warrior."

"Thank you, sire," said Prinsessa, giving Aríel a side-glance of reproof, "but she still needs to learn manners."

"No matter," Kafteinn replied. "There is much to discuss and much to do. We should move away from this dangerous place and head back to the village."

"We need to do something about the children's clothes," said Skessa, thinking ahead.

"We will stop at the farm of Torfi and his family," said Kafteinn. "This family understands us best, and I will also put a little extra understanding in their minds. I will need to cover some of the truth, for it will overwhelm them. So all of you," he spoke directly to the girls, "must be careful of what you say. Do not talk of your home to anyone. This family will understand your purpose when you arrive and will think your clothes odd, but will not understand that you are from the far future. We will get you clothes of our time to wear and hide the clothes of your time. Now mount your horses and they will carry you with the herd."

The girls obeyed, throwing the reins over the heads of their horses and mounting them. The horses mingled with the herd, Hela, Aríel, and Kedja chattering animatedly with the other horses. Prinsessa and Kafteinn spoke privately. The girls sat in their saddles, listening and absorbing their surroundings with interest. In a few moments, Kafteinn gave a shout and the herd started off at a canter, following the river up the valley.

As they rode, Laura saw small movements in the grass. Several field mice and even a small fox hustled to get out of the way of the horses' hooves. Darcy looked over at Kim, who was pointing as a few ptarmigan birds flapped up out of the grass. The two girls grinned at each other and Darcy gave a little nod.

~ EIGHT ~

Laura Makes a New Friend

Emily watched as the plain, river, and mountains sped by. The herd was moving at a great speed, but with true Icelandic spirit, the horses kept the girls balanced and provided an exceptionally smooth ride. She had time now to think and her mind was a blur of events. Only a week ago she had been on the ground of the Klingshern's riding arena, fighting with Andrea. Now they were riding together in Iceland, 800 years in the past, headed into a mission to save a chieftain's daughter while two villages battled over food and horses. What were her parents and the other parents thinking? Her parents seemed fuzzy and the memories of them not quite real. She frowned, wondering why she wasn't more upset about them. A soft voice came into her mind.

"Do not worry, my dear," said Prinsessa, "I have taken care of everything."

Emily leaned forward and saw Kim riding Prinsessa on the

outer edge of the herd with Kafteinn. Prinsessa nodded at her with reassurance. Emily felt the last vestiges of worry dissolving. Too much was happening here, and besides she trusted Prinsessa—if she said it was taken care of, then it was.

She thought for a moment and then said, "Skessa, aren't you getting tired? We've never run so far so fast before."

"No, Emily, we may not have ridden like this, but I have ridden into battle several times and traveled far when I have come to the home of our sires."

"I don't understand—how have you come here?" Emily asked, bewildered. "You and Prinsessa have never been missing from our farm."

"As Prinsessa told you, she has great powers and we journey when you are not aware."

"But we're never apart more than the time we're at school or sleeping. How could you have fought battles in such a short time?"

"Ah, those are part of Prinsessa's powers," said Skessa solemnly. "You will come to understand them soon."

"What about your powers?" Emily asked her, trying to get Skessa to keep talking. She did not appear to speak as much as Prinsessa or some of the other horses.

"Oh, I have powers as well," Skessa told her, sounding matter-of-fact. "Some of Prinsessa's powers are greater than mine, but I have some that Prinsessa does not have. That is why Prinsessa chose me as her aid. She often consults me on her decisions and she does rely on me for my strength and size when we are in battle. I have saved Prinsessa's life at least twice," Skessa bragged.

"Really? That's amazing. You will have to tell me what happened. But for now, can you tell me about where we are going?" Emily asked. "Have you been there before?"

"I have," replied Skessa, "but you must wait and see for yourself. Now please allow me some time to think. I think well when I am running and I have much to think about."

"Oh," said Emily, "I'm sorry for disturbing you."

"You never disturb me," Skessa said with some emotion. "You are a part of me. But sometimes, I must do my thinking."

"I understand." Emily fell silent and just watched as the sea of grass rushed by.

Riding on Aríel on the far side of the herd, Laura observed the mountains closing in on them. The plain was becoming a valley with the river continuing up the middle. They had crossed several tributaries to the river, splashing through without losing speed or time. Ahead she could begin to see changes in the land. A great mountain appeared to rise out of the valley directly in front of them. Closer to the mountain, the vegetation changed— unlike the flat plain, here there were shrubs, heather, crowberry, bearberry and small trees, willow and dwarf birch. Laura also thought she could begin to see signs of civilization. It was not long before they were cantering between fields of wheat, rye, and corn.

Laura could see that the crops did not look healthy, showing the impact the weather had on food supplies. Pretty soon she could see small homesteads made out of stone and wood with turf roofs. Everywhere she looked there were herds of horses. Most of the herds were free and some joined Kafteinn's herd.

Laura rode comfortably on Aríel in her usual posture, back straight, head up, alert to her surroundings. She didn't know what it was, but Laura felt an inner excitement, an expectation that this journey was her opportunity to accomplish something great, that she would do things she never expected she could do and this was somehow meant to be. Laura had always had an inner confidence— she had strong convictions and never followed the trends or fads that everyone else did. If she liked something or believed in it, she did it. If she didn't, she refused to go along. Because she exuded such confidence, instead of being an outsider, others respected her. Laura was not outspoken; she just quietly lived her life according to what she believed and was a well-adjusted, happy teenager. She was beautiful—her thick blond hair and blue eyes and tall athletic frame effortlessly attracted boys, though she found most of the boys her age silly and immature. Laura had no patience for that. She had no patience for the shallowness and superficiality of the Red Carpet Girls either, but so far on this trip, it was looking as if there might be hope for Andrea to turn out to be a decent person after all.

Laura felt the strength of Aríel's muscles beneath her thighs and the clean light breeze against the blond hair on her arms. She closed her eyes and smiled. This was an adventure she would never forget, no matter what happened. She opened her eyes, glanced over and saw Emily watching her. The best friends laughed, enjoying the moment.

Kafteinn was careful to steer away from any human population until he had provided appropriate clothing for the girls. He hadn't gone far before he brought the herd to a halt at the side of a circular group of five small stone, wood, and turf buildings. By this time, there were almost 200 horses with Kafteinn. They all stood around looking innocent and grazing on the brownish grass away from the cultivated fields. A tall young man, who looked about the same age as Emily, Laura, and Andrea, but with an adult air about him, came out from one of the houses. Three shaggy sheep dogs trotted along beside him.

With a sharp intake of breath, Laura watched as he walked toward her with long, sure strides. He was, without a doubt, the best looking guy she had ever seen. His face looked as if it had been chiseled out of marble—he had a strong jaw, a cleft in his chin, and dimple in his cheek. His nose was noble and his eyes a striking blue-green. His hair was a tousled dark blond, falling across his golden tan forehead. He was muscular and fit; he was obviously used to hard labor. All of the girls stared at him with wide eyes. Besides being drop-dead gorgeous, he was the first human they had met in this distant time and place.

The boy walked right to Laura and Aríel. Although he spoke to everyone, his eyes stayed fixed on hers. Laura's cheeks began to flush, but she was somehow able to meet his gaze. The dogs sat down at his feet and waited expectantly.

"Welcome, travelers," he said in a strong, sure voice. "I have been expecting you. My family is out working the fields and they sent me in to meet you."

Laura stared back at him without breathing, wondering why he had immediately singled her out. It was one of the few times in her life she felt shaky and unsure of herself. Her stomach was doing little flips.

Suddenly, all the girls heard the voice of Kafteinn in their head. "Introduce yourself, Laura. And do not worry, he will hear your words as they are said in Icelandic. Ask him where Torfi is."

Laura, uncharacteristically stammering, said, "My... my name is... is Laura. Can you tell us... where is Torfi?"

The boy continued to stare at Laura with intensity and then said, his voice softening, "It is an honor to meet you, Laura. My name is Reynir Torfason. My father has instructed me to find you some other clothes. Why are you clothed so strangely? I have never seen girls in pants, and I am certain I have never seen pants like those before."

"And what do you think of girls in pants?" Andrea spoke up, wanting this good-looking boy to notice her. "Don't you think we look good?" Andrea stood in her saddle and preened for him, smiling and tossing her hair.

"I do not mean to be rude to you, but I am addressing Laura and would like to hear her answer," Reynir barely glanced at Andrea, dismissing her and turning back to Laura.

Andrea huffed back onto the saddle. Kim and Darcy guffawed behind their hands and Andrea glared at them. Emily had to look away to hide her smile. That Andrea! You had to give her points for trying.

Laura, who had been thinking of how to respond to the question, said, "Uh...that's a little hard to explain. We are from far away and we have different customs there. However, while we are here, we would like to dress like the people of your village to honor your customs."

"I can understand that," Reynir spoke respectfully. "You are very thoughtful, Laura. However, I understand you are here to help our people as warriors, so instead of having you dress in women's clothing, you are to be outfitted in men's attire, so you will change from one pair of pants to another." Reynir's eyes sparkled and he leaned in so only Laura could hear him. "And I have to say, in response to your friend's question, you in particular look very fetching in pants, Laura from Far Away. I am glad you are here now." Laura blushed with embarrassment, but smiled.

Resuming his normal tone, Reynir continued, "Come, I have six smaller brothers. You will borrow clothes from them. I have prepared the clothing for you and put them in our home and the home of my father's brother. You can change there."

Laura thought it strange that Reynir was speaking to her as if she was the leader of the group. Just as she was thinking this, she heard the voice of Prinsessa.

"He likes the way you look, Laura. He also sees the gift of strength in you to be a leader."

Laura blushed again and the other girls giggled. Andrea pouted. Emily looked at her best friend with pride. Reynir looked around at them without understanding.

"I'm sorry, Reynir; we do not mean to be rude to you. Thank you for giving us clothes to wear." Laura took a deep breath and mentally accepted her new role as leader.

Reynir nodded at her and their eyes met—there was an air of possibility that lay between them, which excluded everyone else.

"Let me introduce you to everyone," Laura told him. "This is my best friend Emily, and this is Kim, Emily's younger sister." Laura indicated the two. Reynir smiled and nodded at each of them.

"This is Kim's best friend, Darcy."

"Hello," Darcy said shyly, ducking her head when Reynir turned his smile toward her.

"And this is our friend, Andrea," Laura finished.

Andrea leaned forward with a dazzling smile, trying to impress Reynir. He glanced at her politely and then said to the whole group, "I am very pleased to make your acquaintance. Welcome to our land. I believe you are all here for great purpose."

Reynir then took them nearby to the homes of his father and his uncle, where they all dismounted. The girls split up—Emily, Kim, and Darcy went in one house, and Andrea and Laura into the other. The dogs stationed themselves near the doorways and sat down patiently.

Inside the one Emily entered, she saw that it had a dirt floor and only two rooms, but was very neat. There was an area for cooking and eating, and another for sleeping, a very simple layout. Clothes lay neatly folded on tidy straw beds. The pants, made of a rough beige linen material, reminded Emily of loose riding breeches. These tied with a rope around the waist. Then there were tunics that went over them, dyed blue, dark green, bright yellow, and dark red. Reynir had also put out funny dark stockings and soft leather boots.

Emily whispered to Kim, "This stuff is itchy." Darcy heard too, and they both nodded.

The girls had to remove their pants, shoes, and socks, but decided to leave on their underwear and T-shirts, which would be hidden by the ancient clothing and be softer against their skin. They all liked the soft moccasin boots and traded around until they found the best fitting sizes.

Over in the other house, Andrea cringed at the feel of the material.

"I don't like this, it's scratchy!" she complained. "Hey, Xena,

Warrior Princess, can't you see if they have something softer?" she whined.

Laura gave her a fierce look. "Andrea, quit whining and get moving. We have important things to do here. Focus! Oh, and don't forget to take off your watch." Laura noticed hers had quit running anyway.

Grumbling, Andrea obeyed.

Soon all the girls were dressed and had bundled up the clothes they had removed. They all walked outside and Reynir looked at them with admiration.

"Now you look right," Reynir said, staring at Laura, who was wearing a dark blue tunic that made her eyes even bluer. She looked tall and imposing in the clothes, the short trousers hugging her figure, her legs long, showing off the boots, and her blond hair smoothed and re-braided down her back. She reminded the other girls to remove all their watches, earrings, bracelets, and necklaces and stuff them in with their clothing.

"Your skin is very light," the girls heard Prinsessa saying to them, "just as these people, so you will fit in perfectly. Icelandic people emigrated here from many different countries so they have varied hair color and unique looks. You all look just like them. Give Reynir your tack and saddlebags as well. You will ride bareback from here on out."

As Prinsessa spoke to them, the girls looked off into space as if they were in a trance. Reynir stared at them, wondering what was happening, since he couldn't hear Prinsessa communicating with them. Then Laura's eyes refocused as she turned to Reynir and asked, "Is there somewhere we can put our clothing and our saddles until we return?"

"Yes," replied Reynir, "Father told me to put them in Frami's house under the beds. I will take care of them." He took the bundles in his arms and disappeared back into one of the houses, then came back out and made several trips with the saddles and saddlebags.

"When Reynir returns, tell him we must head toward the village without delay," Kafteinn told Laura, who nodded.

She walked to Aríel and picked up the reins, which were lying over her neck while she nibbled grass. As Reynir came back out, she saw him watching her.

"We must head for the village now," she stated with confidence, looking across at him. "We are here for an important reason."

"I know of your mission," Reynir told her. "You have come to rescue Gígja, daughter of Arnþor, our chieftain. You are very brave, and Father has instructed me to help you in the village."

"We are glad you will be helping us, Reynir," Laura told him.

"Yes, thank you for everything, Reynir," both Kim and Darcy chimed in, looking at the older boy with hero worship. He favored them with a smile and they both sighed loudly.

Andrea, who was standing by Emily, looked at her as if to say, we don't need any dumb boy. Emily smiled back and whispered to her, "Let's stick together."

Andrea nodded gratefully. Maybe Emily wasn't so bad after all. She scratched her arm, where it was being irritated by the unrefined fabric.

"All herd," said Kafteinn so all the horses and girls could hear, but not Reynir, "you must stay here until our plans are made. For now Prinsessa, Skessa, Kedja, Hela, Aríel, and I will travel to the village. Angur, you will carry Reynir. The girls will need him to get into the village and announce their arrival to the bishop."

Angur walked over to Reynir, who mounted him without saddle or reins. The girls each mounted their own horses and the rest of the herd continued to munch on the dry grass. Soon the seven horses, hooves pounding, were cantering across the valley. The girls, their stocking-clad legs gripping the sides of the horses and hair rippling out behind them, flew toward the village. Laura and Reynir rode together in front, side by side.

~ NINE ~

The Village of Hólar

As Reynir led the way through the fields toward the village, Kafteinn and Prinsessa talked to the girls. Laura had dropped back a little behind Reynir so she could hear.

"When we enter the village," said Kafteinn, "the people will come out in the streets to see you. We have spread the word of your mission through our minds to the people. You are to show your bravery, but be respectful and polite. There is a family there who has a large home where you will be staying. We will start there and then go to see the bishop. This will be a very difficult challenge, for you must convince him to take you to see Arnþor. Arnþor has refused to see anyone since his daughter Gígja was captured."

"You will bring great joy to the villagers," said Prinsessa, "since the people believe that Arnþor has abandoned them and they are exposed to an attack by Siklingur."

"What are we to do if we get in to see Arnþor?" Emily asked, her brow creased in a worried frown. She shook her red-gold hair out of her eyes and adjusted her stockings—darned stuff was so uncomfortable, they kept twisting around and bunching up.

"This is why I am so grateful that Prinsessa was able to bring you," Kafteinn responded. "I am hoping that when he sees that you are all brave and beautiful like his daughter, he will take heart and come forth to his people. If you are able to accomplish this, then the village will again be defended and we can work on how to save Gígja."

"Kafteinn, you might have made a mistake," Darcy said in a small voice.

"What do you mean, child?" Kafteinn demanded.

"I am neither brave nor beautiful—I'm kind of just a little nerd. I've never done anything courageous before. Maybe I'm not right for this," Darcy said in a small voice, her eyes filling with tears.

"I do not know this word you use, 'nerd', but I believe you to be the one who is mistaken here, daughter. You were brought here because of your gifts and your character—you would not be here otherwise. Perhaps you do not know what these gifts are, but they will certainly come to light and you will live out your journey as it was meant to be. Do not call me wrong—I know beauty when I see it," Kafteinn told her.

"Thank you, Kafteinn. I will do my best, I promise," Darcy stated, looking stronger and sitting a little taller on Hela.

"Yes, stop talking like that, Darcy, or I'll dump you right off onto your backside," Hela said crossly. "You are my rider and I should know—you're worthy to be riding on me!"

"I'm sorry, Hela, I didn't mean anything by it," Darcy apologized. "For your information, people never think they are beautiful!"

"Well, except maybe me and Heather and Erica," Andrea put in ungrammatically, and, to everyone's surprise, laughed at herself.

"Beauty is not always on the outside, you know," Hela informed the girls. "Sometimes it starts on the inside and it radiates out from there."

Darcy thought about this for a minute, and then Emily spoke up.

"Excuse me, but have you given any thought to how we are going to rescue Gígja from a dungeon in a village at the other end of the plain? It must be fifty miles to Akureyri from here!"

"Fifty kilometers from Akureyri to Hólar, and that's if we follow the twisty valley," Skessa corrected Emily, looking back up at her. "Otherwise, it's only about thirty kilometers as the goose flies. I have been giving it a lot of thought, and the first thing we must do is to figure out the layout of the Great House in Akureyri. This is not going to be easy. Even the best of Arnþor's men have tried to get in and failed. Some never returned."

At this, Kim gasped. How dangerous was this going to be? She saw Prinsessa glance back at her and made herself lift up her chin and try to look unconcerned. Her horse nodded in approval and Kim felt better.

"I know that Siklingur has a weakness, but I have not been able to pull it from his mind. He is very clever at hiding his thoughts."

Not much more was said as the group reached the edge of the village. Just as Kafteinn had predicted, nearly everyone came out of their homes and shops to see the girls.

"Hail to these who have come to save Gígja!" Reynir shouted as they proceeded down the street. Cheers started to well up from the villagers. Following Laura's lead, the other girls sat up at attention and began smiling and waving at the people along the way. Prinsessa was able to use her powers to alter the perception of the villagers so that rather than seeing five teenage girls dressed in boy's clothing, they saw the girls' gifts and strengths—what could be and what would be—warriors cloaked in wisdom, strength, and beauty.

The village was a mass of people, strange sights and smells. The streets were crowded with carts, piles of cabbage and potatoes, blueberries, pots and pans, and fish vendors with heaps of haddock, cod, and halibut—every one of them hoping to catch the eye of the customers strolling past. The street was filled with a mix of people—shopkeepers with aprons over their tunics, small children running among the adults, women shopping for goods, babies strapped to their mothers, men smoking and conducting their trades, and there were dogs wandering among them all.

"Whew, someone needs to tell these people about deodorant!"

Andrea covered her nose with her hand.

"And it smells like rotten food and sewage! Peww!" Emily replied, while smiling and waving as if nothing was wrong.

They passed a group of four or five boys their age, who quit kicking around a small bag filled with beans and stared, then started shoving each other and messing around, trying to get the girls' attention. Emily and Andrea smiled at them and gave them a little wave.

Soon they had passed out of the village with its shops and arrived in front of a large house. It looked more like an inn, because it was so much larger than any of the neighboring homes. Reynir dismounted and motioned for the girls to do the same. A stable boy came around to take the horses, but after a whisper from Kafteinn, Laura told the boy that their horses were to go free. The girls removed the horses' bridles and they moved off. There were spacious grazing areas surrounding the village where the herds stayed. Prinsessa, Skessa, Kedja, Aríel, and Hela headed there to join the horses that had welcomed them earlier. The herd was waiting for them in the grazing area nearest the village.

The girls followed Reynir up to the front door. The family, an older man and woman with their adult sons, met them at the door, bowing and thanking them for coming.

The older man stepped forward. "I am Máttur and this is my wife Daria and my two youngest sons, Baldur and Leifur. Three of our other children have their own homes, and our two youngest sons were killed in the battles with Akureyri. We are happy to welcome you into our home. I am sure you are hungry and thirsty after your travels."

Everyone nodded—they were both hungry and thirsty, but the urgency of their plans came first, they knew, hearing Prinsessa's voice as if she was standing in the room.

"We are very thankful for your hospitality," Laura told him, using a kind but firm voice, "and while it is true that we are both tired and hungry, we must see the bishop as soon as possible."

"Yes," Reynir agreed, "it is imperative for them to visit the bishop before twilight falls. We will be back as soon as we have met with him."

"We understand," said Máttur. "Your purpose is of great importance to our village and we will help in any way we can."

Baldur handed Emily a large skin bag of water and all the girls had a long drink of the cold, clear water. It tasted so good that they sighed with pleasure, wiping their mouths with the backs of their hands.

"While you are gone, we will prepare food for you and have it ready for your return. Then you can get a good night of sleep," Daria told them in a motherly way.

Thanking the family, they left their bridles at the house while Reynir ushered them outside, holding the door and resting his hand for a moment on Laura's back as she stepped out in front of him.

As soon as the girls left the house, they noticed the sun was beginning to reach the horizon, although the air remained warm and comfortable. Prinsessa had told them that the sun never really set at this time of the year, but that it did partially dip below the horizon for about six hours. This produced a twilight effect, but not full darkness. They were all exhausted from their journey, since they had been awake for so long. Emily did a quick calculation in her head and figured out that they had not slept in nearly twenty hours. In spite of the powers Prinsessa had bestowed on them, fatigue was beginning to take its toll. Emily shook her head to clear it, but it didn't seem to help.

There were still many people out as Reynir led them along the streets of the village; they were constantly bowed to or patted on the back or cheered. The girls were too tired to really appreciate the admiration and tried to just keep moving.

Suddenly, they could hear the voice of Prinsessa, who was still able to communicate with them from over in the grazing field near the village.

"I know you are all tired and hungry. I will try to give you some energy to stave off your hunger until we see what we can accomplish with Bishop Abel."

There was a silence, and each of the girls began feeling a strange pulse, starting at the tips of their fingers. It radiated throughout their bodies and they all stopped, eyes closed, as they were infused with what felt like light and sound, a burst of energy that woke them up and re-energized them.

"Are you all right?" Reynir, walking a bit ahead noticed when they stopped. He walked back a few steps to Laura. He touched her hand. "Laura?"

Her eyes popped open and she took a deep breath and replied, "Oh yes! I'm fine! Much better now!" She gave him such a dazzling smile that, for a moment, he found himself unable to move. He had never met a girl who was as beautiful and capable as Laura; she had an inner light of grace and confidence. It took all of his determination to concentrate on his duties and what he was supposed to be doing. No one had ever mesmerized him like this before.

"Good, great, now let's go," he told her, forcing himself to stop looking at her and move on.

All of the girls continued walking with a spring in their step that hadn't been there before. They felt as if they had gotten a refreshing nap and had their second wind.

"Now listen carefully," Prinsessa's voice continued where she had left off. "Abel is the only one who can get you in to see Arnþor. You must impress upon him that you have come to rescue Gígja. He is already aware of it, but does not believe it possible. You will need to utilize your powers of persuasion. I have confidence that you can do this—this is why I brought you. You are all very smart and if you work together as a team, I know you will come up with something. I have done just about all I can for you. Now it is up to you."

None of the girls answered. Although they had a good deal more energy than before and their hunger was subsiding, they still had no clue what would happen and felt a bit uncertain. Paired in twos—Reynir and Laura, Andrea and Emily, and then Kim and Darcy—they came to a hill. Emily realized that they were at the base of the great mountain they had seen earlier from a distance. In front of them was a large building made of stone with a thatched roof. The building was the size of a small castle. Although it was only one story, it was spread both long and wide. There were large gates leading into a courtyard. Guards were posted at each side. As they approached, the guards brought their spears up and shouted, "Strangers! Identify yourselves for passage!" The group stopped, Kim and Darcy looking at each other nervously. Reynir stepped ahead and bowed.

"I am Reynir Torfason. We are here to see Bishop Abel. These are the travelers who have come from afar to help with the rescue of Gígja."

The guards scrutinized the girls with narrowed eyes. The look of strength and power Prinsessa had given them was apparently satisfactory; they were admitted and directed to the chambers of the bishop. The girls passed through the halls, mouths open, staring at everything in disbelief. They had never seen anything like this before. It was like being in a castle out of a fairy tale. Great torches hung from the walls and large tapestries that depicted the history of the people were draped over the walls of stone. Sound bounced off the great stone floors and through the cavernous spaces in echoes. Andrea felt very small in proportion to everything around her and craned her neck, trying to take it all in.

Kim and Darcy oohed and ahhed over everything, pointing things out in excited whispers. Their hushed tones could not hide their curiosity and amazement.

Emily looked at each of the people they passed with interest, wondering who they were and what their roles were here. When she saw young women wearing silk dresses with lacy collars, she realized what a shock it must be for the villagers to see teenaged, female warriors walking around. Laura and Reynir walked together, looking straight ahead, focused on the task they were about to face. The two strode purposefully, their steps matched perfectly.

Before long, they came to a great door where another guard stood. He remained silent and simply opened the door and led them into the chamber. An older gentleman with a big bushy head of gray hair sat on a large chair at one end of the room. Unlike their plain cotton tunics, his was made of gold brocade and studded with jewels on the shoulders and arms. He had rings on all his fingers and a heavy cross of silver around his neck. His boots were also lavishly adorned with colorful jewels. As they approached, the man looked up. His eyes were so filled with sadness that Emily found her own eyes filling with tears.

She made herself blink them away.

"How come you to our land and in what way do you think that you can help us?" he asked heavily with no introduction.

Laura, who had approached first with Reynir, spoke up. She had no idea, beforehand, what she was going to say, she just opened her mouth and the words came out.

"Oh, Great Bishop Abel, we have traveled far to this village to bring our many skills to assist in the rescue of Gígja and we hope to bring about the advent of peace."

"Bah!" the bishop scoffed. "I do not care how far you have traveled! You are...you are merely women! What skills can you possibly have that our militia does not already possess?" he sneered.

Andrea, who was used to being a bit of a snob, began to think that she might put it to use and stepped forward with a haughty attitude.

"Great Abel, you have no idea of our abilities. In the land from which we have come, we are respected for our intelligence, strength, and bravery." Her tone dared the bishop to argue with her statement.

Abel looked at the girls standing before him. They had an air of confidence and wisdom about them and all looked straight into his eyes with no sign of weakness or fear. "Hmm, perhaps. But where have you come from and how did you hear of our plight?" he asked, looking at them with suspicion.

There was a momentary silence, and then Emily spoke up. "We have traveled farther than you can imagine. Our hearts are one with the horses of your herds and they are the ones who carried the word of Gígja's capture unto us."

All of them could hear both Prinsessa and Kafteinn groan at this answer, but Emily continued.

"You know well the bravery and strengths of Gígja, yet you question ours?" she said, sounding stern and frowning at Bishop Abel. "She is one of us and we will not leave until we have returned her to her home."

Emily said this with such conviction that the old bishop brightened for a second. A brief smile crossed his face and he nodded.

"It will do Arnþor good to see you. I believe you will restore his hope. You are much like Gígja and maybe he will see a chance to save her."

"Good job, Emily," both Prinsessa and Kafteinn's voices mingled together to all of the girls, "good job to all of you. You have made the first step."

The bishop stood and led the girls down a long hallway; it was dark and scary looking. Dimly lit wall sconces flickered in the distance. Reynir was instructed to stay behind because Bishop Abel wanted the chieftain to feel the full power of the girls' presence. Finally, the bishop and girls came to a wooden door, so small that they all had to duck as they entered. Before them, they saw a man who looked so sad that once again, Emily's eyes filled with tears. Even though he did not look that old, he seemed burdened with a huge weight on his shoulders. As they entered, he looked up at them with dull, uninterested eyes.

For the first time, Kim and Darcy felt that they were needed. Without saying a word, they ran to Arnþor and knelt in front of him, each girl taking one of his hands in both of hers. The moment they had done this, Arnþor's eyes began to clear. He looked at the girls in front of him and then at his bishop.

"You...you all...carry the spirit of my daughter," he said, his voice shaky, but gaining strength as he spoke. "I see it so clearly. I acquired knowledge from Kafteinn that he would bring women from a far off land to help rescue my daughter. Honestly, I did not believe it. The touch of your hands makes me feel it could possibly be true after all," his eyes scanned the brave young women who stood before him. "You are the ones who can save my Gígja."

Andrea, Emily, and Laura stepped forward, surrounding him and placing their hands on his shoulders in a show of solidarity.

"We are here for your daughter," Laura addressed him, sounding solemn. "That is our sole purpose for coming."

Arnþor closed his eyes and smiled.

"Kafteinn is the greatest of my herd and the one that I understand the most. He has done a wonderful thing for me. I must present you to my people and show them that I have confidence in you."

To the surprise of everyone, especially Bishop Abel, Arnþor

stood and took his sword. He then led the girls back down the long hall. Reynir joined them from where he had been waiting, and they all went out onto the steps of the Great House. When the girls had first entered the Great House, word had spread that strangers from far away had arrived. Curiosity drew a large crowd and the twilight was now aglow with torches. When Arnþor came out onto the steps, a great roar came from those who had gathered. Everyone was thrilled to see their leader. Arnþor raised his arm and everyone fell silent.

"My people, I have shut my eyes to you with the loss of my daughter, but now Kafteinn, the greatest horse of my herd, has brought me help unasked for, and in a form completely unexpected. You may see these warriors as women, but I see the free spirit and soul of my daughter in every one. Even the young ones carry a power that will bring us supremacy and success." He held the hands of Kim and Darcy and raised them in the air to the sound of another great cheer.

All the girls could feel the pride of Prinsessa and Skessa. Kafteinn said with confidence, "You have now accomplished the second step and the people have their chieftain back. You girls have done well. Prinsessa and Skessa, you have chosen well. Now it is time for you to get some food and rest."

Reynir said to the chieftain, "Sire, the family of Máttur has agreed to take in the girls. They need food and rest. I should take them there now."

"They deserve to stay in the Great House," Arnþor said, "but Máttur and Daria will take good care of them and they will get better rest in their home. There is much to do this night. I will meet with the leaders of our army. I know that in my sorrow, I have been negligent of my duties. We are fortunate nothing worse has happened. We must be properly prepared. Go, sisters of my daughter. You are in good hands with Máttur. Get food and sleep and come to me in the morning. Praise Kafteinn for the gift of your arrival."

The girls felt exhaustion washing over them in a huge wave. Reynir said, "Come, and stay together."

He led them through the crowd, who crushed close to them, touching the girls and patting their shoulders, expressing their gratitude and good wishes. Reynir took Laura and little Darcy's hands, holding them close in the crowd. Emily, Andrea, and Kim also joined hands so they wouldn't lose each other in the mass of people.

They made it back to the house of Máttur, escorted by many of the villagers, stumbling through the huge door with fatigue. Reynir let go of Darcy, and pulled Laura aside for a moment in the front hallway.

Laura gazed into Reynir's intense blue-green eyes, her hand small and soft in his large calloused one.

"I wish you a blessed night of sleep. Rest well, Laura of Far Away. Know I shall be thinking of you this night," he told her softly.

"Thank you for everything, Reynir. I am very grateful that you were chosen to accompany us. I shall look forward to seeing you tomorrow as well." With a gentle smile, Laura squeezed his hand, stepped away and disappeared into the house.

Reynir sighed and slumped against the doorframe. This was truly the best day of his life; how could tomorrow be any better? Smiling, he shoved himself upright and headed home to sleep.

Inside, the girls noticed that, like the homes of Reynir's family, this house was very simple and each room had a specific purpose. The kitchen was the warmest room and the fire in the fireplace gave off a soft glow. From the rough timbers crossing the ceiling, pots and kettles hung and cast shadows on the opposite wall. The bedrooms were small, with a bed and a table with a bowl for washing. Daria bustled around making sure the girls had what they needed. A great stone table was set with delicious smelling soup, bowls of blueberries, and plates piled high with laufabrauð—paper thin, deep fried bread. Everyone ate ravenously without saying a word. By the time they were finished eating, Kim and Darcy were already dozing, leaning on Emily. Emily and Laura shook them awake and half-carried the two to the rooms that had been prepared for them, setting them gently on the straw mattresses. They pulled off their boots and covered the younger girls with hand-woven blankets. Then they joined Andrea in a bedroom next door. They decided they would sleep better without the unfamiliar clothes, so they stripped off the stockings, trousers, and tunics and collapsed on the beds in their underwear and T-shirts, pulling up the rough blankets to cover themselves. Daria came in and checked on them, making sure they were tucked in.

"I haven't gotten to do this in a while. I wish you blessed sleep." Daria, a round, plump woman, cheerfully smiled and gave them each a pat on the shoulder.

"Thank you so much. Good night," they murmured.

Within seconds, they were sound asleep.

~ TEN ~

We Need a Plan

In spite of the straw beds and coarse blankets, the five girls slept soundly. It had been late when they had collapsed into bed the night before, so it was not surprising that the sun had already risen and was climbing into the sky when they awoke. A constant breeze blew across the town and into the windows where the girls were sleeping, making the temperature very comfortable. The previous winter had been an unusually long one with almost no spring or fall. Going from harsh winter snow and cold temperatures right to hot and dry conditions made both fishing and farming very difficult. Since the girls had arrived in summer, the weather was beautiful—warm in the direct sun, cool in the shade, and always breezy.

Laura and Emily were the first to wake up. After dressing and finger combing their hair, they left their room to find Reynir,

Baldur, and Leifur sitting at the table, talking, having finished their breakfast meal. The room where the family ate was light and bright, with the wooden shutters pushed open and sunlight streaming in. There were sconces on the wall with half-melted candles in them. There was a large, rough hand-carved wooden table and large wooden chairs in the middle of the room, which had been the site of hundreds of family meals.

Daria was stirring a pot of batter at a working table, built with large gray stones at the end of the room. She had already put rye bread, butter, honey, and a plate of cheeses on the table.

"Hail to the heroes," laughed Reynir, a sparkle in his eye as Laura came in, "lazing about. You slept so long that you almost missed breakfast!"

He was sitting at the table with Máttur and his two large sons, Baldur and Leifur.

"We had a very long day yesterday!" Emily stopped, one hand on her hip, sounding a little offended.

"You don't pay him any mind," Daria told them. "You girls needed rest!"

"Hey! Quit it!" Reynir put his hands up to protect his head from Daria, who was flapping him with her apron.

"I was teasing," Reynir apologized to Emily. "I hope the others wake soon. You are all wanted at the Great House."

Laura smiled down at him as she walked by to an empty chair and touched his shoulder. "You be nice!" she told him, sounding severe, but her smile belied her tone.

"I will, I promise!" Reynir grinned at her. Just as he spoke these words, Andrea came in, her hair sticking out in all directions, looking crabby. She was followed by Kim and Darcy. Unlike Andrea, they were wide awake and hopping around like a couple of jumping beans.

Andrea flopped into a chair, her arms folded, glowering at everyone.

"We woke her up," Kim explained.

Daria looked up with a welcoming smile. "Good morning, my dears. Oh! Oh, my! You come with me, Andrea, and let us do something to fix your hair."

Without giving her a chance to say anything, Daria pulled Andrea out of the chair and spirited her away, making motherly noises.

"I hope you slept well," Máttur boomed in a hearty greeting. "Are you hungry?"

"I kept waking myself up when I rolled over on the rope tie of my pants, it's so bumpy!" Kim giggled. "I think I have a permanent dent in my stomach."

Flustered at Kim's comments, Máttur huffed and poked his elbow at his sons, saying, "Get up! Get up! Let us make room so the girls can eat!"

Baldur and Leifur bowed to the girls, smiling in amusement at their antics, then headed out the door to their work.

"I'm so hungry I could eat an ox," Kim announced.

"Sorry, we do not have ox here," Máttur replied in a serious tone. "Our ancestors could not bring them over in the boats and they would not have survived."

"Uh," Kim replied, "I was just making a joke. Bread is fine!"

"Oh, you are in for a treat—Daria's rye pancakes are delicious!" Máttur told them, licking his lips.

"Yum!" Darcy smiled, nodding.

They sat down where Baldur and Leifur had been, joining Emily and Laura in piling their plates with the bread, butter, cheese, and honey until the pancakes were ready. They started eating with great relish; they were so hungry, everything tasted better than normal. Or maybe it was the food that made everything so tasty, Emily thought to herself, savoring the pure, sweet honey on the whole-grained yeasty bread and the creamy tang of the fresh cheese. Somehow, the flavors were sharper and purer than she remembered foods to be—was it because everything was all natural and fresh? Emily abandoned her analyzing and just enjoyed the experience of eating.

Andrea and Daria came back in the room, Andrea's hair tamed into a smooth ponytail and tied back with a string, her face still damp from splashing cool water on it. She seemed to be in a better humor and helped herself to some bread, eating with contentment.

Daria bustled back to her batter bowl. The room soon smelled delicious, filling with the aroma of pancakes cooking.

Emily turned to Reynir. "When is Arnþor expecting us?"

"He sent word for you all to come as soon as you had rested and had food," replied Reynir. "I think he was up nearly all night with his leaders trying to work out plans. Everyone is so excited that Arnþor is back in charge that no one can sleep."

"Your house is beautiful," Laura told Máttur.

Beaming with pride, Máttur said, "Thank you. We are very fortunate to be able to have such a solid house. Do you know that the walls are all a meter thick?"

"Really? Wow!" Darcy and Kim chimed, having just studied metric units in school that spring.

"Is that because it's so cold here in the winter?" Andrea asked.

"Yes," Máttur was enjoying this, "there is wood on the outside, and then inside the walls, we have stones and turf for a layer of warmth, and then this wood that's inside," he gestured to the smooth, golden walls, "is imported from Norway."

The girls all admired it.

"Of course, it is more expensive, so we also use wood we have gotten from the sea for many other things. Some of the houses even have secret passages in between the walls," Máttur leaned forward and told them in a dramatic whisper.

"Really? How cool! Do you have those here?"

"We do not," Máttur shook his head. "I have seven children—they would cause too much mischief if I had to worry who was sneaking through the secret passages at all hours of the day or night." His eyes twinkled and the girls laughed.

"We also have lots of space between the ceiling and the roof, so when all of my children were living at home, we used the lofts above the great rafters for sleeping areas. Now we don't need all that room," he said, thinking of his sons who were killed by Siklingur's warriors.

"Perhaps someday soon you will have grandchildren who will stay there," Emily put her hand over his in sympathy.

"Thank you, my dear, I do hope that is true someday," Máttur told her, patting her hand. Daria nodded, her eyes brimming with tears.

The girls finished their breakfast, thanking Máttur and Daria for their hospitality and exclaiming over the pancakes. They took the time to wash up in cold bowls of water set out for them, and handled other personal matters in the crude facilities of the ancient times.

"Okay," Andrea whispered to Emily, "so it isn't exactly like home, but it reminds me of camping out on a trail ride. I can deal with it."

Emily smiled. "That's true, we just have to think of it as roughing it. You're doing a good job, Andrea. I'm glad you're here."

Andrea looked happier. Emily actually thought she looked better with her hair natural, not all hair sprayed hard as a rock. Her face was fresh and clean without makeup and her clothes were not skin tight everywhere. She looked like a regular, likable person.

"Come on, girls, we've got to get going!" Laura hurried them all to finish up and head over to the Great House. Walking through the fresh, bright morning air, they heard the voices of Prinsessa and Kafteinn, coming from the grazing area to their consciousnesses as they traveled along the streets of the village.

"Did you sleep well, girls?" Kafteinn asked.

Emily, who was getting the hang of responding with her thoughts and not her mouth, said, "Yes sir, very well. Máttur's family is very kind to us."

The other girls agreed. Kim slipped a bit and started to speak out loud, "I don't even" but Darcy elbowed her and she caught herself, finishing, "...remember going up to bed," in her head. Reynir glanced at her with curiosity, but didn't say anything.

"Well now, let's see how smart you really are," said Prinsessa. "We have been listening to the thoughts and conversation of Arnþor and his men all night, and they are confident that they can protect the village, but they still have no idea how to rescue Gígja."

"Prinsessa, we are not warriors, so how can we help with the plans?" Laura asked, matching her strides to Reynir's as they strolled along together companionably, their hands brushing against each other accidentally as their arms swung. Laura's senses were acutely aware of Reynir's physical presence—his lean limbs strong, his hands and arms golden tan from working in his father's fields.

"You have already proven your skills," replied Kafteinn. "You do not know your own intelligence and strength, plus you bring knowledge from the future and I know that you learn much from paintings which can talk and move."

"They are called movies and television," said Skessa. "I have not seen movies, but I do not approve of television. However, I do agree that they may have picked up things which will be new to the warriors and Arnþor."

"Oh, I have seen television and I think it's wonderful!" Aríel burst out with young enthusiasm. "I was standing in perfect line with the window one day," she told Hela, "and I saw part of the most wonderful story of a black horse and her adventures."

"Yes, we know," Hela sighed, exasperated. "You've told us a hundred times—it was *Black Beauty!*"

"And Aríel, how many times have I told you, you are not allowed to watch the humans' television? That is strictly forbidden!" Prinsessa scolded.

"But Mother, it's educational," Aríel whined in a typical teenager's lament. "I'm learning something!"

"Aríel!" Prinsessa said fiercely.

"Yes, Mother," Aríel sounded subdued, knowing she was going to get a lecture later.

Laura, Emily, Kim, Darcy, and even Andrea were laughing at

this whole exchange, finding it very amusing.

"What is it?" Reynir wanted to know, looking around.

"I am sorry, it is just something we girls can share—it is called an inside joke. Please forgive us," Laura told him, her eyes apologetic.

"It is all right. You are from far away, somewhere I cannot know. It is part of your mystery, I guess," Reynir gave her a charming smile, his dimple deepening.

"Yes, I need to keep you guessing a little, so you do not become bored with me," Laura's blue eyes twinkled.

"I could never become bored with you. I am only just starting to get to know you, and I like what I have seen so far. I would like to have a chance to talk to you more."

"I would like that too, but I have no idea when that will be. However," Laura told him, sounding cheerful, "I will look forward to it."

By this time, the girls had reached the gates and now the guards saluted them with their long-handled battleaxes rather than stopping them. There were still many people milling around and an excited murmur spread through the villagers upon their arrival. Again clothed in luxurious garb, a light jewel-studded cloak with a fur collar and a fancy hat, Bishop Abel was waiting at the gate and gave them a warm welcome. He led them to a great hall. Reynir stopped at the door. "I will be back for you later," he told them all, but looked at Laura.

"I will miss your company," Laura said softly to him.

"And I, yours," Reynir replied, watching Laura's straight back and long legs as she led the other girls away.

The room was dominated by a huge, carved wooden table placed in the middle. Many warriors were seated around it. Arnþor, looking hopeful and expectant, was sitting in a big, dark wooden chair at the very head of the table with hand-drawn maps and papers in front of him. As soon as he saw the girls, he stood and opened his arms to them. Kim and Darcy ran to him and threw themselves into his bear hug, smothered by his large robe. The warriors smiled at their leader's obvious fatherly affection for the younger girls. Andrea, Emily, and Laura received very respectful nods from everyone and were directed to the empty chairs positioned near Arnþor.

Once the girls were seated, the chieftain said, "I am so glad to see you today. You are all looking well rested and ready for the challenges we now face. I have something for each of you. Tafar, bring the gifts forward, if you please."

One of the gentlemen seated at the table to Arnþor's left rose and walked into another room. A few moments later he returned, followed by several servant boys, whose arms were laden with swords, helmets, and knives. There were leather jerkins, which were close fitting, hip-length, collarless jackets. They didn't have any sleeves, but did have extended shoulder pieces, and came with belts. They were made to be worn over a tunic, and were used as armor against sword cuts and arrows. The sleeveless style allowed freedom of movement during fighting.

Tafar distributed the items. To Laura, Emily, and Andrea he gave great heavy swords and small, but lethally sharp, knives. Kim and Darcy were also given the small knives. All the girls were given helmets and jerkins.

The girls looked at the heaps of heavy and bulky equipment sitting in piles on the table in front of them and stared at Arnþor, not knowing what to say.

"I am aware that you traveled lightly during your long trip and were limited in what you could bring, but now you are fitted as proper warriors," Arnþor stated with satisfaction.

Laura spoke first. "Thank you, Arnþor. We are most thankful for such fine equipment."

"Yes, thank you, Arnþor." "Thank you." Andrea and Emily chimed in.

Darcy and Kim ran over and kissed Arnþor on the cheek. The other warriors gasped at such brazen behavior, but Arnþor patted their faces, saying, "You are most welcome, little warriors."

Luckily, the girls heard Kafteinn begin explaining to them how to put on the gear and soon they had donned the jerkins and helmets, put their knives in leather holders in the belts of their jerkins and sheathed their swords. There was one funny moment as Andrea put on her helmet. It was far too big for her and she felt as though her whole head was rattling around like an acorn in it. Plus, the metal bands on it were so heavy, her neck felt compressed under its weight.

"Tafar!" Arnþor snapped his fingers, seeing Andrea's trouble. "The head of one of our warriors is too small."

"It is not too small!" Andrea peered out from under the large helmet resting on the bridge of her nose, "Someone else just has a big fat head!"

One of the servants ran to get a smaller one for Andrea and everyone was amused as she yanked it off and pouted until the new one arrived.

"Ah, much better," she said as the new helmet settled neatly on top of her head. "Do I look good?"

The other girls nodded enthusiastically, giggling, and Andrea smiled, satisfied.

As they stood before Arnþor, they heard Prinsessa whisper to them, "Now you are warriors and little by little, you will find you no longer need my power for your strength, bravery, and knowledge. You are creating your own." The rest of the warriors gave a little gasp and stood and saluted the girls.

"Ahh," Arnþor sighed in satisfaction. "I feel as if I have five of my daughters just like Gígja, standing before me. All right, lay your weapons down with your helmets and join us. We need your help."

Emily stood still for a moment, unable to picture herself in a situation where she would need all of this protection and what she would do with these weapons, but had a strange inner sense that once she was there, she would know exactly what to do. She felt the power overtaking her and knew that she was in some way transformed into someone else, someone strong and mighty, when she wore it. As she removed all of her equipment, she felt as though she had shed those layers, and returned to her usual self.

After the girls took off their gear, they laid it carefully under a window on the floor, and took their seats at the large table. They all shared Emily's feelings—that they were no longer strangers or felt out of place, they were truly a part of a great army.

Arnþor began. "My warrior leaders and I have worked most of the night. We have developed a plan to protect the village and lands around it from Siklingur's army. But we have not been able to figure out a way to rescue Gígja."

"Tell us your plan and we will see if that helps us to devise a way to get to her," Laura suggested. Arnþor complied, and the girls listened intently.

Laura leaned forward, her elbows on her knees and her hands cradling her head. As she listened to Arnþor's plan, she was starting to get the germ of an idea. Her inspiration came from a movie she had seen. Inside her mind, she felt Skessa's presence, picking up the thread of her idea and filling out the details.

"What about a diversion?" Laura stood up. "What if our warriors attacked Akureyri? We would not have to use all of them.

Some could stay back here to protect the village, but if we placed the balance of our warriors at strategic locations, then Siklingur's warriors would have to split up to fight back at each location. We could work out places where our warriors could not be fought as a group but would be split up and hidden so that Siklingur's warriors would have to split up even further to find them."

She made a compelling figure in front of the warriors as she paced back and forth along the table, her graceful long body moving artfully, and her silky blond hair glinting in the sun coming in the windows.

"Then," she continued, "while this diversion was going on, another team could sneak into the Great House and rescue Gígja!" Laura looked around the table, breathless with expectation and waited for the response. As she sat back down, Emily reached over and squeezed her hand. The two younger girls looked a little nervous.

Although most of the men had caught Laura's air of excitement, Arnþor and the other warriors forced themselves to think carefully about this idea. After a few minutes, Arnþor said, "I like the concept of what you propose, but there are many details we must work out. And we must not forget, we still have to deal with our worst problem."

"What is that?" Emily asked, her brow lined with worry.

"We do not know where Gígja is hidden now," Arnþor told her, "and if we begin an attack, the first thing Siklingur will do is hide her away and surround her with warriors."

"So," said Laura, "that means we must find a secret way in, locate Gígja, and be ready to take her before the attack begins."

"You make it sound like it is easy," Tafar spoke up, "but we have tried to find a secret entrance and lost many warriors in the process. We have never been able to find any way in but the main gate."

Emily was surprised that they had heard nothing from Skessa, Prinsessa, or Kafteinn during these discussions. She realized now that Prinsessa meant what she said earlier, that both the horses and villagers were depending on them for their ideas and intelligence. Emily thought and thought as the conversation went on, discussing the pluses and minuses of the idea, and finally something came to her. Again, she did not feel Prinsessa or Skessa's influence, which threw her a little.

"What if," she interrupted, and all eyes turned to her, "we mustered the entire herd of horses and had them charge the village and Great House while the warriors drew off Siklingur's army? Several hundred horses charging through the village would cause such mayhem that my friends and I could probably get in the main gate unnoticed and figure out where Gígja is!"

Arnþor considered this for a moment and then said, "Many horses could be killed..." at this Laura frowned "...and there are no guarantees that you would be able to get in the gates or find the dungeons."

"We are very good at handling situations as they come to us," Laura said, sounding firm and sure. "That is why we were brought here. I feel certain that we could work around any problems that arose, though the loss of any horses would be a terrible thing. Anyway, we're good at thinking on our feet."

"It is true," Arnþor was thoughtful in his reply. "We do have options which were not open to us before. But it would take a lot of work to plan."

"Well," Laura wanted to know, "what are we waiting for? Let's get started."

The chieftain, warriors, and girls got down to work. The plan proved much harder to work out than they had originally thought. At one point, scouts were sent out to try to locate places to hide the warriors before the attack.

Food was brought in—great hunks of smoked lamb, platters of duck and goose, herring and shrimp along with other fish, cheese, fruit, and baskets of laufabrauð. The men drank tankards of ale, which the girls were offered and turned down, asking for water instead. The group continued to work as they ate and drank. Kim and Darcy could not help much with the planning and were bored. They asked to go for a walk after they had finished eating. Everyone took a small break after the meal to stretch a bit. Laura, Andrea, and Emily went to use the facilities. When they came back out, Laura spotted Reynir coming towards them. His eyes lit up when he saw her.

"I was just coming to check on you," he called and nodded hello to the other girls.

Andrea and Emily smiled back and continued walking down the hall.

"Hello, Reynir," Laura's happy smile made his stomach do flip-flops.

"Come with me for a moment." Grabbing her hand, Reynir ducked around the corner and part way down the hallway, he pulled her into a small alcove.

"Laura..." Reynir stood so close to her, Laura could feel the cool stones of the wall behind her back and the warmth of Reynir's body pressing up against her. He was warm and smelled of fresh grass and soap. "I am concerned for your safety and the danger of what you girls are doing."

"That is the reason we came here. Do not worry, Reynir; we have many who are looking out for us," Laura told him, thinking of Aríel, Kafteinn, Prinsessa and the rest. Her hands smoothed the front of Reynir's tunic.

"You are the most beautiful girl I have ever seen. I feel connected to you in a way that is different from anything else I have ever felt with anyone. I am very fortunate to know you, Laura. I do not wish to waste an opportunity to tell you how important you have become to me in such a short time," Reynir's voice was husky and Laura caught her breath as he leaned closer to her, cupping her face with his large hands.

Laura could hardly breathe as his lips met hers... her first kiss, she thought, and it was perfect. His mouth was firm on hers, his lips soft and yet strong. As she kissed him back, she felt a tingle spread all the way through her body and she gave a breathy sigh into his mouth.

"Laura! Laura!" The faint sound of Emily and Andrea's voices reached the two in the recesses of the alcove.

"I must go," Laura sighed.

"I know. I am already looking forward to seeing you again," Reynir managed to tell her. She squeezed his fingers and ducked out of the alcove, moving lightly down the hallway toward her friends' summons. Reynir groaned and leaned face forward into the wall. How had he been so lucky as to meet someone as wonderful as Laura? He made himself get moving; the sooner he finished his afternoon's tasks, the sooner he could get back here and see her again. He was already looking forward to meeting the group at the end of the day and providing them his escort.

"Come on, Laura," Andrea waved her over. "Everyone's waiting for us to get started."

"I'm coming!" Laura's secret smile reached Emily in an instant.

Andrea turned and led the way in, but Emily grabbed Laura's arm. "Did he kiss you?" she demanded.

"Yesssss...." Laura looked at Emily dreamily.

"Oh, my gosh, Laura, that's awesome! How was it?"

"Oh, Emily, better than perfect."

The girls resumed their seats at the table, and Laura forced herself to shove all thoughts of Reynir to the back of her mind and concentrate on the strategy and plan for finding Gígja.

Almost all of the warriors had ideas and input for the plan, some pointing out flaws and making suggestions, others spearheading ideas. Laura was outspoken about what she felt the girls' roles should be and contributed quite a bit to the conversation. Emily and Andrea were more reticent, but both of them listened closely, brought up several points that had been overlooked, and offered insight in some areas. Their thoughtful input garnered the respect of the warriors, who acknowledged the girls' wisdom and the value of their words and ideas.

Meanwhile, Kim and Darcy had left and begun their tour of Arnþor's Great House, which he had invited them to explore.

"Man," said Kim after they had walked for a while, "they weren't joking when they called this a 'Great House.'"

"Yeah," replied Darcy, "it's like walking through the Natural History Museum down in Philly."

"Can you believe these tapestries? It's hard to believe these people actually made them by hand!" Kim stopped in front of one and studied it.

"I know, the same with these paintings! It's a lot more interesting seeing it here than in some gallery."

The rooms and hallways were huge, all connected, and just seemed to go on and on from one passageway to another.

"I hope we can find our way back." Darcy was nervous.

"Don't worry, I'm not like my father—I'll ask for directions," Kim told her and they started giggling.

They wandered downstairs to the lower floors. Here they found storage cellars filled with piles of potatoes, beets, turnips, cabbage, carrots, and fruit and large barrels marked Flour and Sugar. They also heard scuttling noises, and Kim jumped about a foot when several mice appeared, running along the edge of the floor. Both girls shuddered and looked away. There were locked rooms which they decided must be dungeons—they pressed their heads up against the doors to see if they could hear any prisoners calling out in agony, but could not.

"My mom always said she doesn't know where I got my wild imagination," Darcy told her, her ear smashed against the door. "My mom and dad are the most practical, boring people in the world."

"You probably got it from hanging around me," Kim said in her usual cheerful way.

They came to other passageways that led to rooms, rooms, and more rooms.

"What the heck do they use all these for?" Darcy wondered, standing in the middle of a hallway, hands on her hips, looking at the rabbit warren of halls and doorways.

They found one room piled high with wood that they figured was used for the fires in the kitchen fireplaces, hallway hearths, and bedchamber fireplaces. There was a slit of light coming from the corner of the ceiling above the woodpile. Darcy climbed up on top of it and reached toward the light. She slid a bit on the uneven wood pieces and her arm banged against the wall.

"Ouch! Whoa... oh, gosh!" she exclaimed, pulling at the crack of the wall and feeling it move a little. "Hey, check this out, Kim!" Excited, Darcy pulled on it again.

"What is it?" Kim asked from below.

"It's a little door. They must shove the wood in here from the outside to store it!" Darcy told her. "I'm going to see if I can fit through it!"

Kim started to tell her not to, but then realized shy, little Darcy hardly ever did anything reckless, so why shouldn't she have a little adventure?

Hoisting herself up, Darcy shimmied and wiggled this way and that, fitting herself into the chute. Finally, panting, she was able to pull herself through and stood up blinking in the outside sunlight. She brushed all the wood chips and big splinters off her clothing.

"Come on out, Kim!" Darcy lifted the chute open a crack and called down to her friend, wood pieces sticking out of her hair.

"I'm coming!" Kim jumped up and worked her way out the door as Darcy had done.

"Hey, look," Darcy said, "I think we're outside the walls of the Great House. Look down there," she pointed. They could see a large herd of horses grazing down at the bottom of the hill.

"There's Prinsessa!" Kim exclaimed.

"Where's Hela?" Darcy shaded her eyes with her hand and studied the herd.

"There she is! Come on!" They ran down the hill and arrived, laughing and breathless, running among the horses to get to theirs.

"Prinsessa!"

"Hela!"

"Why did you not stay with the Counsel?" Prinsessa asked, accepting Kim's exuberant hug, but speaking in a somewhat reprimanding tone.

"Uh, well, Prinsessa, we were getting bored and Arnþor told us it was okay to explore the Great House. We saw you down here and wanted to see you—I missed you. Did we do something wrong?" Kim asked, crushed. Her arms dropped from Prinsessa's neck.

"Prinsessa," Darcy was leaning on Hela's side, "did you see the little door we squeezed through at the back of the Great House?"

"I did," Hela was the one who answered. "I knew those skinny little bodies were good for something."

"That's what I was thinking too, Hela! Maybe," Darcy said triumphantly, "they have a door like this at Siklingur's Great House! If it's like this one and goes right by the dungeons, we could get in there and get Gígja!"

"Darcy, you're a genius!" Kim told her.

"Wait just a minute, you two," Prinsessa's stern tone froze both of them in their tracks. They looked at her intently. "Listen to me carefully. I do not want you to mention this to anyone. It was not my intention for you young ones to even come on this dangerous venture, and you are the only ones who could fit through an opening like that. There is no way I want you so close to the danger."

"You didn't even want us to come, Prinsessa?" Kim asked, crestfallen.

"It's not that I didn't want you to come, Kim—it's just that I want to make sure you are safe and there are times when I cannot protect you. That distresses me greatly. But as Kafteinn pointed out, you are part of a bigger plan, and I therefore agreed to it."

"But," Kim pointed out, still unhappy, "we can be useful—after all, we were the ones who brought Arnþor out of his dark spell."

"I know," responded Prinsessa in a loving but still stern tone, moving toward Kim and rubbing the girl's arm with her neck. "You have accomplished a lot. Arnþor has great feelings for you, but I do not want you to put yourself in any danger from which I cannot protect you. Do you understand?"

"Yes," said the two girls together.

"Well, even though you were worried about our coming on the journey, we are here now, so we should help where we can," Darcy pointed out.

"But..." Hela started.

"Could we ride a little?" Kim interrupted, changing the subject. "Maybe you could show us around the village or something."

"Sure, girls, come on. You don't need any bridles, just hang onto our manes."

"What about the Counsel? Should you be gone that long?" Aríel asked, worried.

"Oh, they're talking about all this planning stuff and what could go wrong and what they should do if this happens, or that happens," Darcy explained, sounding long suffering. "They'll be there all day."

"As well they should," Prinsessa said gravely. "Details are important."

"I know. They're just boring," Darcy said, sounding a little childish.

"How's Laura doing?" Aríel wanted to know.

"She's doing great," Kim enthused. "If anybody can make this work, it's Laura. She's so smart."

"I think she's in love," Darcy sing-songed.

"What? She's not in love! She just met him!" Kim argued.

"It can happen that fast," Darcy told Kim. "I read about it in books all the time!"

Kim rolled her eyes.

"Oh, that's so romantic," Aríel sighed, with teenage envy.

Prinsessa sighed to herself. How complicated was this going to be—Laura and Reynir as two star-crossed lovers? The girls would have to return to their own time eventually, and then what would happen? Prinsessa made up her mind not to worry—there was only so much she could control and what was meant to be was meant to be.

"Come on, let's go already!" Hela urged.

The two girls mounted the horses bareback and grabbed a huge handful of the famous thick, long Icelandic manes and off they went. The horses alternately cantered and tölted around the area outside the Great House and then walked into town, telling the girls all about the history of Iceland and its people.

Many of the villagers who were on the streets, going about their daily lives and routines, spoke to them and wanted a chance to visit, but the horses allowed the girls just to give a friendly greeting and kept them moving.

After that, Prinsessa and Hela moved onto the valley plain. They began to gallop along the river bank moving away from the village. The sun was shining and there was a sweet smell in the air. The girls loved the feeling of speed and freedom as the valley flew past them. They felt so alive and full of energy. After a bit, the two horses slowed to a walk and roamed over to the river for a drink. The girls looked around at the beauty of the snowcapped mountains that ran along the valley. After taking a long and refreshing drink, Prinsessa looked up and noticed the sun beginning to set.

"We must head back," she told the two girls, "the twilight is coming."

"Can we canter back, Prinsessa?" Kim asked. "That was so much fun."

Prinsessa looked over at Hela who gave a little nod and the two horses took off without another word. In about twenty minutes they were back at the gates of the Great House.

"Do not forget what I told you," Prinsessa reminded them, "and behave yourselves. Not a word about the wood chute. Now, hurry along. You are already late for supper and the Counsel is wondering what happened to you."

The two girls hopped off, hugged their horses, and then ran back to the Counsel room.

"Ah ha," Arnþor's face lit up with a smile as the girls came rushing in. "Here are our two missing princesses. I hope you have enjoyed your truancy."

"Sorry, sir," said Kim as she took her seat beside him. "We enjoyed exploring—your house is amazing! Thank you for letting us look."

Arnþor nodded.

"Then we rode our horses around the area to learn more about your village."

"It is wonderful that you took the time to gain knowledge about our land and our people," Arnþor beamed at the two of them, pleased. He called to a servant, "Végeir, bring these girls food and drink!"

"I don't know what it is—the water here is so good!" Darcy said after she gulped the cold, clear Icelandic water.

Emily reached over and patted her sister's arm, glad to see her back safely and relieved that she and Darcy had been under Prinsessa and Hela's watch. She did not like the idea of the two girls running around by themselves in unfamiliar territory.

While Darcy and Kim ate hungrily, the chieftain summarized the plans that had been prepared while they were gone.

"Since we have gone over this many times," began Arnþor, "I will keep this brief. There are details on the maps and documents here on the table, if anyone wants to review the plan before we move forth. For the most part, we have taken the plan devised by Laura and Emily and filled in the details. We need to start as soon as possible to prevent Siklingur from getting any word of it. There are spies everywhere. We must move quickly."

"Tomorrow afternoon," he continued without any interruption, "we will assemble ourselves, our warriors and the herds of horses in the south pasture lands. Just before twilight, we will begin our journey to Akureyri. We will take several rest breaks on the way down. When we are within ten kilometers of the fjord, the majority of the warriors will move on ahead to distribute themselves all around the town. The scouts have identified perfect locations for them to position themselves."

"The rest of us will move on slowly. Laura, Andrea, Emily, and about seven of my warriors will head to the road that leads down the mountain into Akureyri. They will release their horses back to the herd and wait on foot near the village, hidden among the boulders along the road."

"What about us?" Kim interrupted, somewhat garbled with a mouth full of food, "You're not going to leave us behind, are you?"

"No," Arnþor smiled down at the two younger girls. "You'll be with me and my main guard. We'll send the herds of horses with Laura, Emily, Andrea, and the other seven warriors, guided by another ten warriors. They will stay hidden both at the top of the road and out into the valley."

"We will have to hurry to move the warriors and horses around," Laura put in. "Even though we have scouts down there watching for guards and spies along the valley and around the town, we can't be sure that one won't see us and slip through to tell Siklingur."

"You are correct," replied Arnþor. "But there is only one road into Akureyri. If a spy or guard saw us, they would have to take that road. There is no other way into the town except by sea. Our scouts are watching that road with arrows at the ready."

Laura nodded.

"Once all are in place, my warriors, Kim, Darcy, and I will move to the top of the cliff and display a marked flag. This will indicate that I am willing to negotiate," Arnþor explained as an aside. "At that point, Siklingur's guards will see us and scramble to tell him and ready the militia. As soon as we are seen, the horses will be released into the town. They will stampede, with Kafteinn at the lead. This should create total mayhem in the village. As Siklingur's militia come out into the town, they will try to kill the horses with spears to stop the stampede and our hidden warriors will begin firing arrows at them. This should draw them into the hills. The mayhem will prevent Siklingur from maintaining control over his warriors."

"As the last of the horses stampede into the village, Laura, Emily, Andrea, and the seven other warriors will follow the horses into town and use the chaos to work their way into the Great House and release Gígja. This is the part of the plan which we are most unsure of and which will rely on your quick thinking and versatility," he said to Laura.

Laura did not reply. All she heard, echoing through her mind, were Arnþor's words, "They will try to kill the horses with spears to stop the stampede." Looking across the table, Kim noticed a strange look in Laura's eyes as Arnþor talked about the danger to the horses. During the charge, there was a good chance that a large number of horses would be injured or killed. This troubled Kim too, although she suspected the risks could extend to the people as well. However, Kim thought, there was going to be risk involved here—there was just no way to get around it.

"All right, let us be finished here for the day. I think we have a good strategy if we all work together. There are risks, but we will have to overcome them and push forward. I feel very hopeful that we will be successful. Let us all get a blessed night's sleep and convene here tomorrow morning."

With that, Arnþor dismissed the Counsel. The girls gathered up their warrior gear and left. Reynir was waiting for them as they exited the meeting room. He moved to take Laura's gear and carry it for her, but she said, "Thank you, Reynir, but perhaps you could carry Kim and Darcy's things instead." Graciously, Reynir took the younger girls' armsful and escorted them back to the home of Máttur and Daria.

He came in with them, and they piled all their equipment in a spot on the floor of the living space. He bid everyone good night and Laura walked with him back to the front door.

"Even without seeing you dressed for battle, I already know that you are the greatest warrior I have ever seen."

Laura laughed. "What a line! You really know how to charm a girl," she teased.

Reynir looked confused. "I do not understand."

"I'm just teasing you. I may be able to look like a warrior, but we will soon see if I can really live up to your expectations," Laura told him, still smiling.

"You will. Have a blessed sleep. I look forward to seeing you tomorrow, Laura." Because Máttur and Daria were standing nearby, Reynir squeezed Laura's hand, touched her smooth cheek, then turned and left.

~ ELEVEN ~

Laura and Aríel Take a Risk

Everyone had gone to bed and Laura could hear the soft snores of Emily and Andrea near her. No matter how hard she tried, she could not get to sleep. Every time she thought of the horses charging through Akureyri and the possibility of many of them dying to save Gígja, she shuddered. If only there was some other way. She tossed and turned, the straw rustling beneath her, until suddenly, she heard a familiar voice.

"Laura! Laura! I know you are awake! I have an idea! You need to come to me!"

"Aríel!" Laura silently thought back. "Where are you?"

"Just come to the herd! Bring your warrior's gear," Aríel said, obviously excited about something. "South of the village. I will find you."

Laura donned her clothes, then the leather jerkin and weapons Arnþor had given her, fumbling a little in the darkened room. She had taken out her long braid, but didn't want to take the time to redo it, so she just caught the long crimped strands back and tied it with a string in a long ponytail that fell almost to her waist in a wavy mass. At one point, Andrea mumbled and shifted. Laura froze, not moving until she heard Andrea's regular breathing again. She slipped out of the house, making sure she didn't make any noise. She was a little concerned that she was going to be in danger—why would Aríel tell her to bring her weapons and protective gear? Nervous, she kept looking around as she headed south, but all seemed quiet. The twilight glow allowed her to see fairly well where she was going. As soon as she had left the outskirts of the village, she heard the clatter of Aríel's hooves and her horse came running up. Laura gave her a hug and then said, "It's good to see you, Aríel. I missed you today. Is everything okay? What's going on?"

"I know exactly how you feel about the plan," Aríel told her.

"I don't want any horses to die, especially you. For the life of me, I can't come up with any better ideas."

"Well, we're both brave and smart, aren't we?" Aríel said stoutly. "I believe that if we leave right now we could catch Siklingur and his warriors off-guard, sneak into his Great House, and rescue Gígja."

"Are you crazy?!" Laura cried, aghast. "That's a very risky and dangerous move. I can't believe you're even here—can't Prinsessa hear us? How'd you even get this far?"

"No, she can't hear us," Aríel replied, a little stung because Laura didn't immediately embrace her plan with great enthusiasm. "I am using some of my own powers. I have been practicing. No one can hear us. Now, come on. No one is expecting this, so it's a foolproof plan. Word has to have leaked out that Arnþor and all his warriors are planning something and were planning it only today. They won't be expecting you at all, and that's the best time, when everyone's guard is down."

Laura recognized the validity of this argument and stood thinking, the sword heavy on her hip.

"Laura, do you really want to see so many horses die?"

"No, of course I don't!" Laura said, sounding cross. "All right, I'm not promising we'll do it, but let's at least ride down there and check out the situation."

"Yes!" Aríel enthused.

Laura jumped on Aríel a bit awkwardly, still adjusting to her gear. She was barely astride when Aríel took off like a shot toward the sea. Laura hung onto her thick mane with one hand and her helmet with the other as Aríel thundered along at a gallop.

"Now, Aríel, although I said we'd see what we can do," Laura said, passing her thoughts to Aríel as they sped along, "we need some sort of plan."

"Well," Aríel spoke as if she were standing in a field, just grazing, rather than galloping down a valley, "I think we can reach Akureyri by early morning. Your coloring and your features make you look so much like a native here, I think we should sneak around and see if we can find some clothing which would make you look like a servant. Then when the gates of Siklingur's Great House open, you could go in with the other servants and pretend that you work there."

"But wouldn't someone notice me?" Laura pointed out. "I mean, they must know who their own servants are."

"I will use my powers," Aríel told her, sounding sure of herself. "I can put out the perception to others that you belong there. Anyway, Siklingur's Great House is so huge that once you are inside, you can sneak away into some hall or alcove until everyone scatters and then start your search."

Laura's face warmed as she thought that hiding in an alcove was not going to be nearly as much fun this time as it was before, with Reynir pressed up against her, kissing her softly. She smiled and forced herself back to the present.

"What are you going to do?" she asked. "I thought there weren't as many horses in Akureyri. Will they recognize you or will you give us away?"

"I will hide behind the Great House," Aríel told her. "The closer I am to you, the stronger my powers for you will be. I don't want to get too far away from you. Also, I am going to try to penetrate Siklingur's mind barrier. He's just got to have some weakness that we can use to our advantage."

Laura was not completely convinced yet, but felt that Aríel did have some good arguments, and perhaps she needed to give this a shot in order to protect the horses. She and Aríel talked some more, then fell into silence as Aríel galloped through the cool twilight night.

. . . .

The two arrived at the cliff near the village of Akureyri a little before daybreak. During the ride, Laura had actually been lulled to sleep and gotten some rest; she now felt energized. The sun was still just behind the mountains, providing some concealing shadowy areas, so Laura did not feel exposed. She dismounted, hopping off of Aríel's back, light on her feet. The two walked to one side of the cliff and then down the road lined with birch trees and willows, which followed along the lower slope of a mountain to the town below. There was almost no activity as they quietly entered the village. They stuck to the dark shadowy areas, trying to remain unobtrusive. Pretty soon they could see the Great House and the guards, standing stiffly at attention on either side of the gates. Although Laura had said she would check out the situation and then make a decision, once they had arrived, it was just assumed between Laura and Aríel that they were going ahead with the plan. Aríel felt convinced that Laura was going to be at risk anyway, and that the risk would be lower since no one had any inkling that a rescue attempt would be made now and with just one person. Aríel was also overly confident that her newly acquired powers would be able to handle anything that arose.

They turned back into Akureyri and started wandering through the streets, glancing into yards and common areas as they went by. This was a fishing village with equipment and gear piled by many of the houses—rods, poles, traps, piles of nets, baskets, and clothing hung out to dry. It wasn't long before they spotted a whole family's laundry, including a rough handmade dress hanging on a rope line between two small houses. The crude dress was perfect. It belonged to a large woman, so it fit well over Laura's jerkin and weaponry.

Laura pulled the dress over her head and then she and Aríel made their way back to a secluded spot where they could see the gate of Siklingur's Great House. A little while later, a horn sounded and men and women started walking from the village houses toward the Great House. At the same time, the gates began to open. Laura looked at Aríel.

"Are you ready?" Aríel asked.

"I'm ready," Laura told her.

"Okay, I am going to change the perception of the people so you appear as one of them, a servant arriving to work for the day. Here goes." Aríel became silent and Laura could almost feel her concentrating fiercely as she exercised her new powers.

"I think it's working," Laura said.

"I just hope it lasts," Aríel told her, breathless. "Well, you better get going. I'll be around the back of the Great House over there."

Laura nodded, gave Aríel a hug and then casually stepped out and joined the line of people walking toward the gate. Aríel made her way through quiet streets to the back of the Great House, then blocked out everything else and focused her mind on Laura.

As Laura walked through the gates, her stomach felt jumpy and nervous, but she tried to appear confident and sure, as if she belonged there. Aríel's powers must have worked on the people's perceptions, because the guards never even gave her a look. She followed the other servants into the main hallway of the Great House, and then as they began to split up and head to their respective duties, Laura began to look for an empty hallway or room where she could hide. It wasn't long before she saw a corridor leading off to the left that looked dark and empty. Aríel, who could still feel everything that Laura saw and did, pushed as much power as she could out to her to make everyone in the Great House not notice the girl in the baggy dress. It worked; Laura slipped into a deserted hallway without being noticed.

~ TWELVE ~

The Big Mistake

Emily woke up early on the second morning. With a big yawn, she turned her head and looked around. Next to her, Andrea was lying flat on her back, snoring with a little bit of a wheeze. Laura's bed was empty.

"Good morning, Skessa, Prinsessa, Aríel, Kedja, Hela, and Kafteinn," she thought brightly, sending her silent communication to them, "and good morning to all you other horses." She didn't want to leave anyone out. As she sat up, stretching, she received a collective greeting back from several dozen of the horses and smiled.

Emily got up and pulled on the stockings, her trousers, and laced up her soft boots. She used a hairbrush Daria had given the girls to share and brushed the tangles out of her hair, wondering if there was time to rinse it. She was used to shampooing, conditioning, and blow-drying every day.

She went into the gathering room where Daria was bustling around getting food ready. Emily took a big sniff. Whatever was cooking smelled really good, sweet and yeasty. Máttur was seated at the head of the big table, his usual spot, and Baldur and Leifur were also there, eating heartily. Darcy and Kim, also up and bored with wearing the same clothes, had switched tunics, so that today Kim was in Darcy's red tunic and Darcy was wearing Kim's yellow one.

"Good morning!" She greeted everyone with a smile.

"Blessed morning to you, child!" Daria turned from where she was mixing something in a bowl by hand. "I hope you slept well."

"I did," Emily nodded.

"Is Andrea still sleeping?" Daria asked.

Emily nodded. "Where's Laura?"

"We have not seen her yet. Is she not still sleeping?" Máttur asked.

"No, her bed was empty when I woke up." Emily replied, beginning to feel uneasy.

"Perhaps she is with Reynir?" Daria suggested, a twinkle in her eye.

"No, his younger brother came by with a message that Reynir was needed in the fields to help his father this morning and would be over later," Máttur frowned, beginning to feel concerned for one of his charges.

"I'm sure she's fine—she's probably slipped out to use the

facilities and will be right back. Come, wash up now and have some breakfast," Daria told her, sounding firm.

Emily obeyed, going to the washbasin, thinking, everything's fine. By the time I have washed up, Laura will have come back from using the facilities. Of course, that's where she is.

But she returned and Laura had not come in. Emily ran out and checked for herself. No sign of her friend.

"Where could she have gone?" Kim mumbled through a huge mouthful—Daria was serving kleinur today—hot, yeasty, and seashell shaped—similar to doughnuts. Darcy and Kim were stuffing their mouths full of the sugary treats.

"Now, let's not panic," Emily tried to sound calm.

"Maybe she went to visit the horses," Darcy put in.

"Of course, yes, that's probably where she is!" Emily exclaimed, relieved.

"Come on, Emily, let's go and find her," Kim said.

"I'm coming too," Darcy stated, pushing back from the table and brushing the sugar off her hands.

"All right. We'll feel better after we find her," Emily told them. "Come along!"

"I am sure all is well—do not worry," Máttur told them.

"Thank you, Máttur. Thank you, Daria!"

They all hurried out the front door, reassuring each other that Laura was surely visiting with the horses, but they hurried as they headed toward the grazing field.

When they arrived, Laura was nowhere in sight. Prinsessa, Skessa, Kedja, Hela, and Kafteinn rushed to them.

"Aríel and Laura are gone and we think they are in trouble!" Hela burst out.

"What?" Emily cried. "Where?"

Darcy and Kim gasped, looking stricken.

"Hela!" Prinsessa reprimanded her. "You do not need to blurt out everything you are thinking!"

"I'm sorry," Hela hung her head, chastened.

"Aríel apparently snuck away sometime last night. But I cannot contact her, and I am concerned that there is a problem," Prinsessa told them, distressed. "I am trying to see Laura, but something is blocking me and I cannot reach her."

"Where could she have gone?" Emily cried.

"Laura was very upset with the plan," Kim spoke up. "She didn't like the risk of the attack with the possibility of a lot of the horses getting injured or killed."

"You don't think she went to try to get Gígja out by herself, do you?" Darcy was aghast.

"That," Emily stated, "sounds exactly like something Laura would do."

. . . .

"Okay, Aríel, I'm in. Now, where do you think I should start?" Laura asked, pulling the side of her borrowed dress free where it was caught on the haft of her sword and was bunching up.

Aríel, who was beginning to tire from the new use of her powers, answered, "Well, we know the dungeons would be down below, so I guess you should look for a way to the lower levels."

"Okay," replied Laura. She stuck her head out a little into the hallway and peeked around. Two maids were walking down the hallway away from her, carrying rags and a bucket. They disappeared through a large door. The coast was clear.

"Be careful, though," Aríel warned. "I can feel my powers weakening. Try to stay out of sight."

Since Laura had no idea of the Great House's layout, all she could do was guess. She decided to continue down the darkened passage that she had first chosen. She could feel doors on either side but there were no torches to light the way. She couldn't tell if the doors led to another passage or to a room. She decided not to try the doors, but continued to follow the hallway, wide and cool, with stones bumpy beneath her soft leather boots. She had not gone far when the passage came to a dead end, with two hallways going in opposite directions. She stopped, making sure she stood up against the wall to stay out of sight, looking down the hall to the left. She felt a little fresh air coming from somewhere. She also thought she saw a small flicker of sunlight. Then Laura looked down the passage to her right, and saw that that passage was almost totally dark and smelled damp and musty. She decided to take that one.

Meanwhile, up behind the Great House, Aríel was trying to split her powers. She wanted to keep track of Laura, and at the same time, her mind searched and searched for Siklingur. At first, she looked for some sign of Siklingur himself but then she realized that he had an ability to shut his mind up tight. Perhaps she should look for human servants who were close to him. This proved easy—in a few moments she had found a woman servant who was bringing him food, but to Aríel's frustration, there seemed to be no speaking between them at all. At least she was pretty sure she had pinpointed his location—now she had to see if she could penetrate his mind.

·········

Laura continued along the dark passage for about twenty feet, stumbling a bit in the dark. Soon she found that this hallway had split as well. "How do people find their way around in here?" she muttered to herself, stopping to regroup and figure out which way to go. To the right, one passage went back toward the main hallway, but ahead Laura could see that the passage she was following turned into a set of stairs. Now she could see a flicker of light below her. She crept down the stairs carefully, stopping to listen for any noise and holding her sword against her so it didn't clatter or clank. Finally, she reached the bottom, exhaling nervously. At the bottom of the steps on the right, the passage opened up into a large area. Up and down the passageway, candles burned, set into wall sconces, providing spots of light. Being cautious, Laura peeked around the edge of the stone wall and saw a pile of large barrels and wooden boxes. The candles were set far enough apart that there were a lot of shadows and dark spots. In one corner, Laura could see a big pile of split logs, and realized it must be a storage spot for firewood. There was no one in sight. At the end of the room, to the left of the direction she had come, she could see another passage, but the lighting was so dim, she couldn't make out any of the details of what was down there.

"Ariel!" she called her horse with her thoughts. "I think I may have found something! I'm down in the cellars and there is a passage at the end. Can you tell me anything?"

"Good," came Ariel's faint reply. "Laura, my powers are getting weaker, so there is not much I can do for you, but I have my mind locked onto the place where Siklingur is. I am going to try to break through to him. I have to concentrate as hard as I can, so I may lose touch for a while. Can you hide out and wait for me so I can help you?"

"It's okay," Laura reassured her, buoyed by the fact that she had not seen anyone so far and was feeling confident. No one suspected her or was even looking for her! "I am going to keep going. I will get back with you in a bit."

"Laura... I don't know... what if...?" Ariel sounded even fainter and a little panicky.

"Just concentrate on Siklingur. Don't worry, I'll be fine."

Laura slipped out into the room and darted from shadow to shadow. She stopped every few feet to hide behind a stack of barrels or crates and then looked around and strained to hear anything. There was no one there, as far as she could tell, and she made it to the passage undetected.

Peeking around the corner and into the passage, she saw a line of rough heavy wood doors on both sides of the passage. Each door had a small opening about five feet off the ground. There was another small opening at the base of the door. Immediately, Laura realized she was in the right place—she had made it to the dungeons! The upper opening in the door was used to let the guards look in on the prisoner, and the lower opening was used to pass in a bucket of food or water. There were a lot of doors lining the hallway. Laura didn't want anyone in the dungeons to see her and call out to her. She decided to walk down the center of the passage and take a look into each upper opening as she passed. Her plan was to move rapidly and stay in the middle so it would be difficult to see her from inside the cells.

She took a deep breath, steeling herself, and thought, "If Gígja's down here, I'm going to find her!" She allowed herself another few seconds to think of how proud Reynir would be if she was able to rescue Arnþor's daughter. She imagined him congratulating her with a huge hug and kiss. Shaking the image away, she also thought that it was better to keep Emily, Andrea, Kim, and Darcy from danger too, so she just had to pull this off!

Laura then took one more look around and started down the passage, turning her head from one side to the other as she moved. All the rooms must have had an air passage in the far wall that led to the outside, because each one was lit with a little sliver of daylight. Fortunately, it was just enough for Laura to be able to see vague shapes inside. Every cell Laura glanced in had more than one person in it, and she could pretty much tell that they were all men. A few held low, desultory conversations as they lay on mats on the stone floor, some looked as though they were sleeping, and others sat motionless, staring at nothing. She tried to move faster in case one of them happened to be looking out of the opening of the door. Towards the end of the passageway, she discovered that the last four cells were empty. She stopped at a solid stone wall which marked the end of the passage and turned. Hmm. Where could Gígja be? Had she missed her? Laura felt a crushing disappointment; Gígja must be being held somewhere else in the Great House. No, it would be harder to protect her there. She just had to be down here. It had to be one of the four cells that appeared empty.

She stepped up to the door on the right closest to the wall. She peered in the opening and saw no one but whispered, "Gígja!" No answer. She went to the door next to it and tried again. Again there was no answer. Next, she went across the passage to the door right across from the one she had just tried and tried a third time. "Gígja!" Still nothing. With a defeated sigh, she went up to the last door, the one on the left up against the stone wall. She whispered in the opening, "Gígja!"

To Laura's great amazement, a small voice came back, "It is Gígja—who calls for me?"

"Gígja! Oh Gígja, my name is Laura and I have come from Hólar for you!" Laura whispered breathlessly.

Suddenly, a beautiful young woman's face popped up right in front of Laura at the opening of the door.

"Oh, geez! Don't scare me like that!" Laura gasped, taking a step back and clutching her heart. She glanced around furtively to see if anyone had heard them. The passageway remained quiet.

"Sorry," Gígja giggled. "I just cannot believe my good fortune! Laura, Laura, you have come to help me? Where did you come from? How did you get in here? Look at you! You're a teenaged girl just like me. I don't under…."

"I don't have time to explain, Gígja," Laura interrupted her, whispering furiously. "You have to stay totally quiet—we don't want anyone else in these cells to hear us. I just need to get you out of here."

Gígja got a hold of herself, although Laura knew she was bursting with questions. As Gígja spoke, Laura could immediately see the resemblance to Arnþor's strong spirit in this daughter.

"The keys are at the other end of the passage," Gígja told her briskly. "They are hanging on the left wall as you are going out over there by the stairs. But I must warn you, they will be bringing the first meal of the day at any moment!"

"Okay," said Laura, "I can hide until ..."

"Who goes there? Stranger! Identify yourself!" A voice shouted from the other end of the passage.

Oh no! Laura was so focused on Gígja, she had not noticed two guards who had come down the stairs and were looking her way. Sure enough, they had a large tub of something and a stack of clay bowls that they were going to ladle the food into and pass through the doors to the prisoners. Oh, Laura, fatal mistake! She cursed herself. Lost focus and forgot to account for the time of day and what would be happening!

Gígja's face had fallen, crushed with disappointment, as she heard the guard's voices and realized the jig was up and her hopes of escape were dashed.

Laura hurriedly glanced around her and then looked back at Gígja. "I'm trapped," she told Gígja, "but don't worry, there is more help coming." Gígja felt a surge of desperate hope and peered out as best she could while the guards ran down the passage toward Laura, swords drawn and looking menacing.

Laura threw out the strongest message she possibly could towards her horse. "Aríel...Aríel are you there? Aríel, I am trapped, I need you now!" Unfortunately, there was no response to her desperate plea. Aríel was either totally focused on Siklingur or her powers had ebbed.

At that instant, the two guards reached her. For a moment,

they said nothing, staring at her and assessing the situation. Was this a friend who had somehow come in? A servant who had snuck down and become friendly with Gígja, bringing her food and treats? A traitor to Siklingur? Surely not a rescue attempt—this was a beautiful young girl, not a scruffy, scarred warrior. Laura stared defiantly at the two men who were looking at her so intently, trying to figure out what was happening.

The next thing she knew one of the guards noticed the unnatural bulk beneath her dress. His eyes narrowed and he reached over and grabbed a handful of the fabric covering her clothes. With a quick yank, the dress tore and she was exposed, armor, weapons and all.

"A spy! Seize her!" cried one of the guards and the two grabbed her arms, holding them painfully behind her back.

By this time, all of the other prisoners had gathered around the openings of their cells and began calling out, yelling and making all the noise they could. The chaotic rise of voices bounced off the stone walls, echoing in an unearthly maelstrom of shouting.

"Stop! Silence!" the guards yelled in vain.

As Laura was half-pulled, half-dragged down the passage, the guards squeezing her arms unmercifully, she turned her head and saw Gígja's face in the opening, tears running down her smooth porcelain cheeks as she reached a hand out through the small opening. "Laura!"

"I'm sorry," Laura mouthed before one of the guards yanked her head around.

She was dragged up the stairs, banging her shins painfully on the stone steps, and back into the main hall. They went through two more passages and a door. The next thing Laura knew she was thrown to the floor in a clatter of armor, her sword catching a bit and dinging on the ground and her helmet, which she had been clutching, falling and bouncing away with a clang! Her hair had come undone from its loose string and flew over her head in a blond mass, obscuring her face as she fell forward, landing hard on both palms as she reached out to break her fall. All she could see in front of her was the image of a man sitting in a large chair. Siklingur, she thought.

"Well, well, what have you brought me?" the man in the chair demanded.

"Sir, we have apprehended a spy!" The guard bragged. "She was found in the dungeons, dressed in false servant's clothing and speaking with Gígja!"

Siklingur's fingers drummed on the arm of the chair as he contemplated the girl who had been dumped in a heap on the floor in front of him. The only sound in the room Laura heard was her own uneven breathing, loud and panting.

⋯⋯⋯

Aríel had been concentrating all her efforts, focusing on

Siklingur and had therefore been completely unaware of what was happening to Laura. She knew that Siklingur had moved to his main hall and was sitting before a group of advisors and servants and all were partaking in a huge morning feast, large platters of fish, meat, fruit, and laufabrauð laid out upon on a large table. She was pleased with herself for having found him and felt she was becoming more successful with her powers.

Suddenly, she felt a disruption in the minds of all the people who were in the room with Siklingur. Next, like a beacon of light piercing through the darkness, a blast of evil thoughts came from Siklingur's mind and poured into Aríel. Her mind was almost overloaded, and she gasped as she saw, from Siklingur's eyes, Laura lying on the floor in front of him. Oh, no! The thoughts coming from Siklingur's mind were focused on the girl and they were so horrid that they made Aríel shudder. She had found the weakness in Siklingur's mind, but lost Laura at the same time. With the very last of her reserves, Aríel sent forth a mighty blast of power, and called Prinsessa.

"Mother!" Aríel reached for Prinsessa, penetrating across the fifty kilometers that separated them.

"Aríel!?" came the very disturbed response.

"Mother, I need you! I have found Siklingur's weakness, but Laura has been captured and thrown at his feet! Mother, help me!"

"My God," was the response from all the listening horses.

~ THIRTEEN ~

The Plan Is Set in Motion

Prinsessa looked up at the three girls. "Laura has been captured by Siklingur."

"What!?" everyone chorused. Emily staggered and took a step back. Skessa came over to Emily and nudged her way in, brushing up against her for comfort. The younger girls looked horrified.

"She and Aríel took it upon themselves to attempt a rescue on their own. Aríel has been using her powers to hide this from us and now she is so weak that only I can hear her."

While the girls tried to grasp this news, Prinsessa fell silent. She was communicating with Aríel.

"Daughter, there is no time. We must act immediately. Tell me what you have found out about Siklingur and what they are doing with Laura."

A faint response came back. "Mother, I am so sorry, this

is all my fault."

"Stay focused now, daughter," Prinsessa said sternly. "You are fading by the minute. Tell me what you can before you can no longer communicate."

The response grew weaker and weaker as Aríel answered. "I have seen into Siklingur's mind. It was exposed the instant Laura was thrown at his feet. His mind was opened at the sight of Laura's beauty and youthfulness. Mother, his thoughts were evil. I cannot repeat them. Mother, we need to…" her voice trailed away and was gone.

"You must go to Arnþor right now and tell him what has happened," Prinsessa commanded Emily.

"But what exactly has happened?" Emily asked.

"Yes, tell us!" Darcy and Kim chimed in.

"As I have told you, Aríel and Laura went to Akureyri to try to rescue Gígja. They hid their plan from me and now Laura is in the hands of Siklingur. Aríel is so weak that she cannot communicate with me anymore. One thing Aríel told me before we lost contact was that the instant Siklingur saw Laura, his mind opened."

"But that means Aríel has finally penetrated his mind," Emily interrupted, "and has seen any weakness that is there! Isn't that a good thing?"

"Yes," Prinsessa was reluctant to admit, then added, "but that weakness was exposed when he saw Laura."

"I don't understand! What does that mean?" Emily struggled

against tears that were threatening.

"It means," Prinsessa said quietly, "that Siklingur's weakness is with beautiful, young women. I do not need to say anymore."

"Yes, you do! What do you mean?" Kim cried, not understanding.

"He finds great pleasure in putting his evil hands on them."

"Oh, no," Kim and Darcy breathed in a whisper.

"Oh, Laura!" Emily cried. "We've got to get to her and help her! We cannot allow this to happen! Prinsessa!"

"Emily!" Prinsessa scolded. "Get hold of yourself so we can help Laura. If Laura has opened his mind then I can see into it, but I must concentrate. Once I have seen what I need, I will assemble the herds and have them ready. Go! Go and get Andrea and then go to Arnþor. Now!"

Without another word, the girls turned and ran.

·········

Laura pulled herself to her knees, her palms scraped and stinging. Then she flung her curtain of heavy blond hair back and looked at Siklingur in defiance. He was a petite man, perched on a large elaborate throne and lavishly dressed in silks and jewels. Because he was small in stature, Laura thought he looked like a little boy in a grownup chair. He had golden locks of shiny hair, a bow-shaped mouth, and a scar that ran through his left eyebrow. Although his features were almost...well, pretty...for a man, there was a look in his dark eyes that conveyed power and lust. Two servant girls stood behind him, hands at their sides and staring straight ahead, registering nothing, as they had been trained to do.

Siklingur stared at Laura, assessing her, for several moments. Something about his stare made her tremble, although she steeled herself so she wouldn't let it show.

The room had fallen dead quiet as Laura's sudden arrival had disrupted a lively discussion with Siklingur and his advisors. Siklingur broke the startled silence. His voice was loud and he sneered as he spoke.

"You fools!" he said to the guards and everyone else in the room, sweeping them all with a sarcastic glance. "This is not a spy! It is a gift from Arnþor. No longer do we need to capture beautiful young women from Hólar. Now they are coming directly to us!" He tossed his head back and gave a hearty laugh. To Laura, it sounded deep and evil. All of his advisors joined in the merriment. As he threw back his head, enjoying himself, Laura reached down on her left side and in a flash, grabbed her sword and pulled it from its sheath. She jumped to her feet, switching the sword to her right hand and held it pointed at the chieftain. She cocked her head and assumed a defiant stance, glaring fiercely at Siklingur. This caught everyone off-guard; she truly looked like a warrior. There was a little gasp from some of the people in the room, and a few drew back a little, but Siklingur just looked at her with an amused smile.

"Oh, watch out, my friends," he said sardonically, "our little bee comes with a stinger."

"I can only hope my stinger finds its way straight into your heart," Laura snapped back.

Siklingur laughed again. "Guards, take her to the northeast quadrant. There is a cozy corner room there with a nice view. Make our visitor comfortable," he said in a voice dripping with sarcasm. "Bind her well. Heh, heh, we don't want her leaving us too soon, now, do we?" he said playfully, shaking his finger at Laura.

As he was speaking, the two guards who had brought her in grabbed her arms. The one on her right squeezed her arm so hard, Laura was forced to let go of the sword, which the guard grabbed from her.

"Ouch!" she glared at the guard.

"Careful. Don't put too many marks on that pretty arm," Siklingur warned. "Bind her tight," he repeated in a cold voice, "bind her arms, bind her legs, bind her waist, and bind her neck. That way I know she'll be waiting for me when I come for her."

Laura's stomach quailed when she heard those words and vowed to herself that she would be long gone before Siklingur found her trussed up like a Thanksgiving turkey.

The guards dragged Laura roughly off to the room Siklingur had designated, making their way down a long, wide hallway, through common areas, down another passageway, down another hall, off to the left, through a large sitting area, and down more hallways. Servants bustling about, performing their daily duties, stopped and stared, startled, at the guards dragging the tall blond stranger, dressed in trousers and a jerkin, her beautiful face twisted with worry.

The room the guards entered was clearly a guest chamber and not a prison. Sunshine and fresh air poured in through the four open windows of the corner room. The large room had a high bed with huge carved wooden posts and a tapestry bedcovering. A big stone fireplace graced one wall, and in the sitting area under the window, there was a round table and four chairs. There was a trunk at the end of the bed and another table with a washbowl and pitcher on it. A small covered bucket that served as a chamber pot, was shoved under the edge of the bed.

The guard threw Laura face down on the bed, dropping her sword on the floor, then bound her as Siklingur had instructed. They tied her up with a thin coarse rope that cut her skin. After they bound her feet together and tied her hands behind her back, they ran a piece of rope from her feet to her head, then around her neck. If she tried to move, the knot around her neck would tighten and choke her. Finally, they blindfolded her and flipped her over on the bed. One of the guards ran his hands up and down Laura insolently. Laura stiffened and thrashed, but doing that cut off her breathing. She forced her body to relax.

"Knock it off, Tjörvi—Siklingur don't want you messing with his goods."

"Just checking the ropes. Besides, he'll never know."

"Siklingur knows everything, ya fool."

"And I'm going to be sure to tell him!" Laura spit out.

"You keep your trap shut, girl!" He cursed, and Laura could hear the swish of fabric as he raised his arm. She expected him to strike her at any moment.

"Let me go and I won't say anything—I'll just sneak out of here. Come on, untie me. You don't want to lose your job—or your head—do you?" Laura argued.

"We're not lettin' you go," the other guard answered. "It's your word against his—you think Siklingur's going to believe you? Ha! Tjörvi, we don't need no trouble—you can stop and visit that chambermaid you've been chasing around. Let's get out of here."

Laura could not move or see, but she could hear as the guards laughed together, making ribald remarks about the chambermaid. Their footsteps faded as they left the room and she heard the keys jingling as the door locked from the outside.

· · · · · · · ·

As soon as Emily, Darcy, and Kim ran back to Máttur's house to get Andrea, Prinsessa focused all of her mind and powers on Akureyri. It took her only a few seconds to find Siklingur. While he was looking at Laura, his mind stayed wide open. Prinsessa dove in like an eagle. She had only a few seconds to get the information she needed, and the second Laura was removed from the room, Siklingur's mind snapped shut. Prinsessa then focused on Laura. She saw her being dragged through the Great House and into the guest chamber. She assessed the situation and searched for something she could do to help Laura. While the guards were tying Laura up, Prinsessa used her powers to focus their minds exclusively on the rope. Because they were concentrating on that, they did not discover the knife attached to the rope belt of her trousers and hidden under the jerkin. She had a quick jolt of worry and a flash of anger when the one guard ran his hands over Laura's arms and back, but Prinsessa gave him an extra burst of distraction and that worked. The knife remained unnoticed. Their nudges and remarks about the chambermaid as they were leaving also caused them to forget all about Laura's sword on the floor. So far, so good, she thought.

Prinsessa then turned her focus to Laura's mind.

"Laura, my child, be calm. I am here."

At the sound of Prinsessa's voice, Laura felt her stomach-wrenching fear subside. Prinsessa was here. Everything would be fine.

"Prinsessa, I am so worried about Aríel. What happened? Is she all right?"

"Aríel overdid it—I know she was excited about using her powers, but she overestimated her abilities," Prinsessa said severely.

"I know, but is she all right?'

"She will be fine. If she rests for a time, she will recover. I am sure she will find a place among the few herds there and hide herself until she has the power to communicate with me."

"Well, that does make me feel better, but Prinsessa, I failed," was Laura's calm reply.

"No, Laura," replied Prinsessa. "I am very proud of you. Although you do not know it, you have actually accomplished a great thing. While you stood before Siklingur, behaving as a true warrior would, his mind was open and I was able to search it for clues."

"So you were able to find his weakness?" Laura asked, beginning to feel Prinsessa soothing the pain from the cords around her wrists and neck.

"You are his weakness, my dear, and when you are in his sight, he loses control of the barrier surrounding his mind."

"I am glad, Prinsessa, that I could give myself up for the good of the people and the horses."

"Oh, for goodness' sake, Laura. You are not going to give yourself up," Prinsessa said, impatient.

"Will you make sure that Arnþor gets the news that I have seen Gígja and spoken with her? Tell him she appears to be in good health."

"Yes, I will make sure he knows. All right, now, I want you to listen and do exactly as I instruct you. Twist your left hand to the left and feel at your waist. Do not move the rope up or down."

Prinsessa had numbed the pain from the bindings and Laura was able to move her left hand a bit. Suddenly, she felt something hard.

"My knife!" Laura told Prinsessa. "They didn't take it!"

"Yes, I was able to distract that insolent guard when he ran his hands along your back," Prinsessa said with disgust. "Now if you shift your weight a little to the right, the handle will come out from under your jerkin."

"I have it," replied Laura, as she maneuvered her body and felt the handle between two of her fingers.

"Pull on it slowly," said Prinsessa, "I will continue to numb the pain. You should be able to draw it into your right hand."

Laura did as she was told. She winced a couple of times as a stab of pain slipped through Prinsessa's power. In a few minutes, she had the knife in her right hand and she started sawing at the rope that gripped her neck. The knife was sharp and the thin, coarse rope broke apart after three good pulls.

Laura took in a deep breath. "Ahh, I got the rope off my neck, Prinsessa. What a relief!"

"Good! Keep going, there is no one nearby and I can see that Siklingur is still in his main hall."

In a matter of just a few minutes, Laura had cut all of her bindings and sat up, rubbing her wrists and ripping off the blindfold. She swung her legs over the side of the high bed and hopped off it. As her feet touched the floor, she heard a clang and looked down.

"My sword!" she gasped.

"Yes," said Prinsessa, "I distracted them from the sword as well. Now pick it up, stand up, and swing it with all your might."

Laura picked up the sword and moved away from the bed into the middle of the room. The bright sunshine streamed through the open window and she stood in a strong ray of light. The sword flashed in the sun. Laura brought the heavy weapon up. The muscles in her arms stood out with the effort. She swung it across in a large arc, wondering what would happen. Suddenly, the sword felt as light as a feather in her hand. Almost as if her arms were responding by themselves, she swung it to and fro then cut in and out and under like a professional swordsman. Swish! Swish went the sword in an artful motion, and Laura's feet planted themselves automatically in a defensive stance. Laura was so surprised that she almost dropped the weapon.

"How am I doing this?" Laura gasped, thrilled and amazed. "I feel as if I've been sword fighting all my life!"

"I have given you a gift," said Prinsessa somberly, "and you will need it."

. . . .

Emily, Darcy, and Kim flung the door open and rushed headlong into the house, startling Máttur and Daria, who dropped a plate of kleinur on the floor and clutched her apron.

"Sorry, Daria!" Emily ran through the gathering room toward the room where Andrea was sleeping, the younger girls on her heels. "We have an emergency—we must get Andrea!"

Leaving their hosts staring after them, mouths open, they pounded through the hall and burst into the room Andrea, Emily, and Laura shared. Andrea had just gotten up and was pulling on her trousers, looking grouchy.

"What the..." she was so surprised as the other girls banged the door open and ran in that she lost her balance with one leg caught in the pants and one out, toppled over, and fell on her sleeping mat.

"Andrea—get up! Get dressed!" Emily started pulling on her arm and Andrea struggled like a beetle that had fallen on its back and couldn't get up.

"What? What are you talking about? What's wrong?" Andrea asked, cross. "Stop pulling at me!"

"It's Laura—she's in trouble and we have to help her!" Darcy exclaimed and then burst into tears.

"What? Where is she?" Andrea's expression instantly turned to concern and she righted herself, sitting up, and pulling on the trousers.

Emily explained what they had found out while Kim comforted Darcy. Andrea was appalled.

"I can't believe she'd do that—oh, well, yes, I can—but still, oh, my gosh, and in danger from that horrible man—we've got to go get her! Where's Aríel—is she okay? Oh, if anyone hurts Laura, I'll..." Andrea balled up her fists and looked as if she was ready to do battle right then.

"I know, I know!" Emily sighed. "We've got to go talk to Arnþor right away—come on, hurry, do something about your hair— here," Emily grabbed the brush and started yanking it through Andrea's snarls.

"Ouch, quit it—give me that! Geez, Emily. Go down and ask Daria if she'll wrap up something for me to eat on the way—we'll need our strength if we're going to get Laura out of this mess. Well, go on! Move it!" Andrea told her impatiently. Emily was just standing there staring at her.

"Yeah, that's a good idea." Emily regained control of herself and started toward the door. Then she ran back and grabbed Andrea in a quick hug. "Oh, Andrea, I'm so glad you came— you really have turned out to be a friend, and someone I could trust with my life!" Emily ran down the hall, calling for Daria.

"Darcy! Kim! You guys go get your warrior gear. We better take it along. I don't know what we're doing, but we might need it. I'll gather up Emily's and mine and meet you in a few minutes. Darcy, don't worry—we have a problem, we're going to figure out a way to fix it," Andrea told them.

The younger girls felt calmer with Andrea's take-charge attitude and went to get their equipment.

A few minutes later, they were hurrying toward the Great House to find Arnþor, Emily and Andrea munching on still-warm kleinur and carrying a skin of water. Daria had given them a package of dried meat too, which they would need for energy.

"What about Reynir?" Emily mumbled through a big mouthful.

"Maybe someone can go get him once we get up to Arnþor's," Andrea suggested. "He's going to be pretty upset."

Emily nodded. Both girls felt awkward and weighed down by the unfamiliar swords hanging off their side. Their helmets were bulky and tucked under their arms. Their jerkins felt constraining and a bit too warm, given everything they were carrying and their hustling pace. Darcy and Kim had a lighter load. Although they were also wearing the jerkins and helmets, rather than the large swords, they had just their small knives tucked at their sides.

Heads turned as they passed, villagers out conducting their daily business or headed into town for shopping, wondering what the girls from Far Away were doing with all of their fighting gear and protection. Their perceptions were of four warriors striding confidently, sure of the mission they were on, and the villagers felt reassured.

Just as they were approaching Arnþor's Great House, Prinsessa's voice came to them and they all stopped in the middle of the road.

"Girls, I have spoken to Laura and she wishes you to tell Arnþor that she has seen Gígja and spoken with her, and that she is in good health."

"How is she? What is happening?" Everyone wanted to know.

"I cannot take the time to tell you now—she is all right and I am trying to help her, so I must go. Just pass the message on to Arnþor," Prinsessa instructed them.

"We will, Prinsessa," Andrea answered and they all started walking again, feeling better knowing Laura was all right and that Prinsessa was in contact with her.

Close to Arnþor's Great House now, Emily called to the guards, "Tell Arnþor we are here and take us to him immediately!" The guards took one look at the four girls, dressed for battle, and sent a runner into the Great House to alert the master.

"Come with me," one of several guards outside the gate commanded and led the way. They had just reached the large room where they had planned their strategy only yesterday, when Arnþor came rushing in. He looked harried, his tunic fastened crookedly and his hair mussed.

"What is wrong? What has happened?" he asked, frowning. Darcy and Kim stepped up to him and he put an arm around each one, holding them to his side.

Emily set her helmet on the huge table and sighed, running a hand through her silky red-gold hair. "I'm afraid we have bad news, Arnþor."

"Is it Gígja? What is wrong? And where is Laura?"

"That is the trouble," Andrea told him. "Last night, Laura snuck away and went to Akureyri. She thought she could rescue Gígja, but instead, she has been captured and now Siklingur has her."

"Oh, oh, no!" Dropping his arms from Kim and Darcy, Arnþor clutched his chest and dropped heavily into a chair.

"Arnþor—are you all right?" Kim cried.

"Yes, child, yes," Arnþor patted Kim's hand, trying to rally. "Thank you for your concern."

"We do know Laura has seen Gígja and she is well," Andrea said, setting her helmet next to Emily's.

"That is wonderful news," Arnþor let his breath with a whoosh and some of the color returned to his face. He pounded his fist on the table, startling everyone.

"Our plan is ruined," Arnþor said darkly. "Now we must start all over again."

"No!" Emily exclaimed. "We must implement the plan immediately. Laura did accomplish one thing, and that was a way to learn what Siklingur is planning. I can't explain in detail, but we are sure of the plan now and we must proceed."

Arnþor looked at her in surprise. "Emily, if you have an inside source, I should know about it. After all, it will give us an advantage and flexibility to change our plan as necessary."

"All I can tell you is that the horses are mustering under Kafteinn and they are ready to move," Emily told him. "We must get the warriors ready right away and start down the valley."

"You speak with confidence, Emily and I bow to your knowledge. Time is of the essence. Brynja, blow the Horn of Gathering and summon all of my warriors here immediately!"

A servant boy who had been standing nearby turned to run off, but Darcy blurted out, "Wait!" and he stopped, uncertain of what to do.

"Somebody should go to fetch Reynir. He was supposed to be here, but was needed in his family's fields today."

"Yes, of course. Brynja, make sure someone rides to the Torfi's farm for Reynir," Arnþor commanded.

"Yes, sire," Brynja took off like a shot down the hall.

Within a few moments, from the steps of the Great House, they heard a great horn blast across the town—the call for everyone to assemble.

The next hour was a flurry of chaos and rushing about, leaders pouring into the great hall, warriors assembling in a large field next to the village, plans spread and reviewed on the big table as they waited for everyone to arrive and get equipped for the journey to Akureyri. Andrea, Emily, Darcy, and Kim alternated between helping them with the plan, answering questions, and giving input, to worrying about Laura and the uncertainty of what was going to happen.

Reynir arrived in a breathless rush, bursting into the room.

"What has happened? What is the news of Laura? Why did she go to Akureyri? What was she thinking?" Reynir clamored for answers.

"Reynir, Reynir, calm yourself, son," Arnþor told him.

"Laura was very upset about the possibility of there being a lot of injuries or deaths to the horses when we attacked," Kim explained. "The welfare of the horses is very important to her."

"So she and Aríel left in the middle of the night and rode to Akureyri," Emily picked up the story.

"To try to go after Gígja by herself?" Reynir asked incredulously, grabbing Emily's arm.

"Yes, she actually made it to Gígja, but then she was caught and now Siklingur is holding her captive," Andrea finished.

"Oh, Laura!" Reynir groaned, falling into one of the chairs at the table and holding his head in his hands.

"We will be leaving for Akureyri as soon as we are ready," Arnþor told him. "You need to go with Brynja and get armor and weapons."

"Yes, yes, of course. Thank you for sending someone for me."

"Laura will be most anxious to see you, I am sure," Emily told him, her eyes twinkling.

For the first time since his arrival, Reynir smiled. "And I, her," he murmured.

The entire army assembled outside the village at the end of the valley. Arnþor took the lead position, with Kim and Darcy on his left, Emily and Andrea on his right, and his personal warriors following close behind. Next came the warriors, who would fan out and hide in and around the village of Akureyri. The warriors who would lead the horses into the town came next in the traveling party. Reynir rode with that group. Everyone was on horseback. Three hundred Icelandic horses brought up the rear. They were split in two groups—the Hornafjörður horses went first—that breed was larger and had more endurance and courage. They were followed by the Svaðastaðir horses—a breed that had an attractive gait (completely useless in this battle strategy) and were more dainty and frisky, but provided a physical presence and would participate wholeheartedly.

Arnþor was dressed in battle gear and riding Kafteinn. He turned and rode up and down the ranks of men. With a powerful and commanding voice, he shouted, "You all know why we are here. The girl from Far Away, Laura, attempted to spare us this attack and tried to save Gígja last night on her own. She was captured and is now in the hands of Siklingur. Not only must we save these two, we must bring this conflict to an end once and for all. Siklingur is an evil chieftain and if we dethrone him, the people of Akureyri will choose a new leader who will want peace with Hólar, God willing. Warriors, this is the most important battle we will ever fight, and the good Lord has brought us gifts to help us succeed."

Arnþor returned to the head of the army, sitting high on Kafteinn. "Do you want to save Gígja and Laura?" he shouted, his voice carrying cleanly through the crowd.

A giant roar of accession came from the army.

The hair on Emily's arms stood up—it was such a thrilling moment.

"Do...you...want...peace?!"

Another great roar came, with the warriors' arms lifted into the air for emphasis, waving spears and battle axes wildly, their shields glinting in the sun. This time, Andrea, Darcy, Kim, and Emily joined in as well, screaming, "Yes!"

"Then let us ride and give our all!" With this declaration, Arnþor turned and Kafteinn took off at a gallop with the army and the horses following him with determination.

~ FOURTEEN ~

The Great Battle and Rescue

Laura sat on the bed for a few minutes, wondering what to do next. The door was locked. She went over and peeked out the window, but there was no way out. Even though it was only one story, the Great House was so large that it was still too high up to jump out, and the stone walls made it impossible to get a footing and climb down. She had a moment of excitement when the idea came to her of using the ropes she had been bound with, but when she picked them up, they were far too short, even if she tied the severed ends back together. Disappointed, she hopped back up on the edge of the bed, massaging her wrist where her skin had been rubbed raw. After a minute or two, she thought of trying to reach Ariel. She knew that her horse was weakened and might not be able to hear her, but it was worth a try.

"Ariel! Ariel!" she called to her.

A very weak and worried voice came back. "Laura, are you all right?"

The only reason Aríel could still communicate with Laura was that they were very near to each other. Aríel did not have to push her thoughts far.

"Yes, Aríel. Prinsessa found me and she was able to help me. She distracted the guards so they overlooked my weapons and she numbed the pain from my bindings so I was able to reach my knife and cut the ropes away. The best thing is she gave me the power of swordsmanship. I can handle my sword now as if I have been using one all my life! It's really cool!" Laura grinned.

"Oh, this news is such a relief to me," Aríel whispered. Laura could barely hear her. "I must rest now and get my strength back."

"Are you safe?" Laura asked, anxious about her friend.

"Yes. I have found a small herd that was stolen by Siklingur's spies from Hólar. They knew my mother so they welcomed me. I told them of our plans and they were very excited about the potential for returning home. I am going to hide in the herd for a couple of hours to restore my energy and get my powers back. Let me know if anything is happening. I will sleep now."

"Get some rest, my friend," Laura told Aríel. While she was disappointed that Aríel wasn't strong enough to do anything to help her, she did notice that there seemed to be a little bit of strength already returning to her horse. She just needed time to recharge.

Laura was worried about what to do and what might happen with Siklingur, but she also felt very tired. She did not know how long it would be before her captor came looking for her. After thinking a little longer, she came up with an idea. She gathered the rope she had cut away and then lay back down on the bed. She placed her knife in its scabbard and placed her sword just under her right side so it was hidden but not uncomfortable.

"Yeah, that's all I need is to lie on my sword wrong and cut myself in half by accident," she muttered, adjusting the angle of the blade away from her a little more.

She then arranged the ropes across her legs, neck and stomach so it looked as if she were still bound. She tucked her hand under her side, wrapping her fingers lightly around the haft of the sword. The feel of it comforted her, and the calm feeling Prinsessa had passed to her still lingered. She closed her eyes and in a few minutes, fell asleep.

. . . .

It was hours before the army neared the end of the valley. They had only taken brief rests and switched among a canter, a tölt, and a walk so they would not wear out the horses. They made good progress and by 1:30 in the afternoon, they could see the mountains spreading out, as they followed the twisted valley and river that led to the fjord. As they neared the fishing village, the ground they were traveling on changed from hard, dry grasses to coastal terrain, sedge grasses, bogs and marshes that they had to bypass. Seabirds such as eider duck, arctic terns, guillemots, cormorants, gulls, puffins, and plover roosted nearby, some flapping frantically when startled by the riders, and the air smelled of fish and brine. Out in the water, large flat rocks poked up out of the water. Thousands of seals lounged about on the rocks, covering their surfaces. About a kilometer from the cliff, Arnþor brought the army to a halt.

As soon as they stopped, Prinsessa called to Aríel, "Daughter, can you hear me?"

"Yes, Mother," came the strong reply, "I have been able to rest by hiding in a herd who were stolen by Siklingur from Hólar. I have been watching over Laura. She has made herself to look as if she is still tied up. She has been asleep for hours and Siklingur has not been near her yet."

"This is very good, daughter," replied Prinsessa, relieved. The rest of the girls could hear the conversation and felt better.

"I have also been trying to listen to those advisors of Siklingur whose minds I can enter. I know they are in the Great Hall with him and they are planning something, but I am not sure what," Aríel told Prinsessa, frustrated.

"You have done well, daughter. Stay where you are and keep an eye on Laura. I will see if I can determine what is going on around Siklingur. I will tell you when we are ready to attack."

. . . .

Siklingur had been very busy with his own plans. The capture of the young female spy both pleased and confused him. Why would Arnþor be sending women as spies? Were they being sent as decoys to distract him? Should he be extra vigilant? He had a strong feeling something was afoot, and as soon as Laura had been dragged away, he turned his attention to his advisors to devise his own plans. He had decided it was time to conquer Hólar once and for all. After he had taken some pleasure from this new girl, he would move north with his army, along with Laura and Gígja. When they arrived at Hólar, he would give Arnþor one last chance to give up his village. Arnþor was sure to refuse, at which point Siklingur would kill the girls in front of everyone and proceed to attack with all his forces.

Since Laura's capture this morning, Siklingur had been toying with the idea of having Gígja taken to the room where Laura was being held. Then he could have the pleasure of two young captives. It was a delightful scheme, but he was hesitant. Truth be known, he had avoided Gígja since her arrival. There was something about her that made him uneasy and he didn't know what it was. He knew her father had some unusual powers of magic, especially with the horses. Did she have some of these same powers herself? Perhaps it was the way she looked at him when he went to see her—she drew herself up and gave him a haughty piercing stare that made him feel as if he was a piece of horse dung on the bottom of her delicate slipper. Most people recognized Siklingur's dominant power and authority, but Gígja—that one made him feel insignificant. There was just this look in her eye when she glared at him, as though she could see right through his soul. He did not like that. He was Siklingur—chieftain of a large and well-organized village—he wielded his power over many and all rushed to do his bidding and respected his leadership abilities.

Siklingur did not understand it but admitted to himself that he was afraid of Gígja. Pah! He would just as soon kill her and be done with it.

Throughout the morning, Siklingur had met with his advisors and leaders working out a plan. A little after they had stopped for a large midday feast, he had decided that the plan was nearing completion and he informed everyone that it would be set to take place in the morning. At this news, heads nodded and tankards of ale were raised in approval. His chest swelled with pride.

Now he felt the urge to go to the girl spy. Basking in the glow of his people's respect, Siklingur hopped off his large chair, flinging out his fur robes behind him and strode majestically out the door. He left his advisors and leaders finishing up the plan and headed towards the northeast quadrant—to Laura.

Servants bowed or curtseyed as he made his way down the long hallways and passageways. He nodded back, acknowledging his workers' respect. Finally, he arrived at the room where his captive awaited him. Perhaps this girl would recognize his great power and give him the attention and admiration he was due. At the memory of her long blond hair, startling blue eyes, and graceful figure, Siklingur rubbed his hands together in anticipation, smirking. He reached up to a hook next to the door, hoping no one saw that he had to stretch up on his tiptoes in order to reach the key.

· · · · · · · · ·

As soon as Laura heard the jingling of keys at the door, her eyes popped open, wide awake. She felt very strong and rested. She moved her right hand, which was tucked under her, tightened her hold on the sword and closed her eyes, forcing herself to take light, even, breaths.

Siklingur opened the door and saw a figure lying on the bed. His mind opened wide. Prinsessa and Aríel, who had been focusing on Laura, saw their opportunity. In that instant, Prinsessa jumped into his mind. Aríel joined her.

As Siklingur stood looking at Laura, he realized he was not looking at a virginal young girl. Instead, he was looking at a powerful warrior sent from heaven. A golden aura surrounded her, lighting the bed and the air above her body. Her beauty was unsurpassed: her blond silky hair glowed as though a light shown from within her; there was not a single flaw in her perfectly molded facial features. Her arms were a light golden color and the hairs on her arms didn't just look blond, but appeared as though they had been sprinkled with gold dust. The glow surrounding her was mesmerizing. Was she some kind of goddess?

Siklingur walked up as close to the bedside as he dared, awestruck. Laura kept her eyes closed. She could feel the enormous power that Prinsessa and Aríel were radiating through her—she was a quivering mass of energy, waiting to burst forth.

Just as Siklingur reached out a hand to touch her, his whole arm trembling, Laura's eyes flew open. With one lightening quick move, she sat up and with a swish that cut the air cleanly, the sword flew up at Siklingur's throat. Unfortunately for her, Siklingur reacted by instinct and ducked back, so Laura only nicked him, just a surface wound across his throat. Blood beaded up. Siklingur, gasping, was unable to look away from the intense blue eyes trained fiercely upon his. He staggered back in shock, grasping his throat with one hand, not sure what had just happened and afraid his whole head would fall off. Laura stood up, an unearthly look in her gaze, the golden light still surrounding her. Wielding the sword with one hand, she took one step toward Siklingur. That was it for him. He screamed, stumbling backwards, then found his footing and ran out the door. Laura heard him fumble with the key, but he managed to get the door locked before she could get to it.

. . . .

Meanwhile, Arnþor made arrangements with his men, and Aríel and Prinsessa relayed what was happening to the girls. Darcy and Kim clung to each other, gasping in excitement and horror as they listened. They oohed and aahed, wishing they could have seen Laura's golden aura for themselves.

As soon as Siklingur made his hasty exit from Laura's room, his mind snapped shut. Prinsessa and Aríel had no more access to his thoughts.

Prinsessa then turned her attention to the current plan, which had already been set in motion. Arnþor had deployed the warriors to their hiding places surrounding the village. He then sent Andrea, Emily, Reynir, and the warriors to their position. They were going to enter the Great House on the tails of the stampeding of horses.

"Go as quickly as possible, and be safe!" he told them.

Emily nodded. "You as well, Arnþor."

"Thank you, child."

Emily reached out for Kim and drew her sister into a hug.

"You going to be okay?" she asked.

"Sure, Darcy and I will be fine. We're going to help Arnþor,"

Kim hugged her older sister back.

"Yeah, we have a plan!" Darcy put in.

"What? What kind of plan?" Emily frowned.

"We just told you," Kim said calmly, glaring at Darcy. "We're going to help Arnþor!"

"Hmm, okay," Emily looked from one to the other at their innocent expressions, wondering. "You guys be careful. Do exactly what Arnþor tells you. Don't get into trouble. Look what happened to Laura," she cautioned.

"We'll be with Arnþor—what could happen?" Kim shrugged her shoulders.

Emily hugged Darcy too and then mounted Skessa. With a wave, she rode off. When she glanced back, Arnþor was standing looking after her, a fatherly hand on each of the girls' shoulders. Emily felt comforted; he'd look after them.

"All right, girls, let's get going so we can do our part," Arnþor patted both girls shoulders, then added, "We're going to ride up to the top of the cliff." He mounted Kafteinn and signaled his warriors to follow.

"You almost blew it," Kim muttered to Darcy.

"I know. I'm sorry. I just got excited and blurted it out," Darcy apologized.

"C'mon, stay back a little bit."

Kim and Darcy let Arnþor go ahead and dropped back. Arnþor was concentrating on carrying out his strategy and didn't notice.

"Prinsessa," Kim thought, and both Darcy and Hela could hear, "we need to go with Emily and Andrea."

"No!" Prinsessa commanded. "As I told you before, I do not want you near any danger."

"But, Prinsessa," Kim reasoned, "we know how to get into the lower levels of the Great House without having to go through the gates. You know that! We can go down the wood chute and get Gígja when they start the attack and everyone else is going to get Laura. Why risk Emily and Andrea even more by trying to rescue Gígja when we can do it?"

"Well, it is true," Prinsessa sounded thoughtful. "Aríel told me Laura saw the wood pile near the dungeons. And we do know exactly where Gígja and the keys are."

"Yes," Darcy put in, "and if you get us to the chute at the back of the Great House, you can focus on Emily and Andrea and give them the power to get to Laura."

"They can do it, Prinsessa!" Hela added.

"All right, little daughters," Prinsessa acquiesced. "Your powers of persuasion are good and I can see the reasoning here. Come on, Hela, let's get down to where the others are hiding. We will position ourselves slightly above them so Emily can't see Kim. I do not wish to worry her, or have her take steps that would destroy the entire plan. We must go quickly. The herds are getting ready for their stampede."

Kim and Darcy looked at each other, smiling. This was so

exciting!

Hela and Prinsessa moved away from Arnþor's team stealthily, and then cantered to the road down to Akureyri. The others had already hidden themselves and sent their horses back to the main herd. Prinsessa communicated with Skessa and Kedja, telling them of their plan. She did not tell Kafteinn for fear he might not approve and cause Arnþor to bring everything to a halt.

Just as Prinsessa and Hela found a large opening in the rocks to hide themselves, they could hear Arnþor's great horn from the top of the cliff. The plan had begun.

·········

Siklingur staggered back down to his main hall. Everyone could see the slash across his throat and wondered what had happened. The chieftain was savagely angry; his whole body was shaking with rage as he climbed into his chair. A servant rushed to get bandages and salve for his wound. Siklingur would have liked to arm himself and go right back and kill Laura on the spot, but he was terrified at the golden specter that surrounded her, and frankly, he was afraid to go back in there. With those kinds of supernatural powers and the fact that she towered over him to begin with, he admitted to himself that the odds were stacked against him. Instead, he looked at his line of personal warriors and ordered: "KILL HER!"

There was a little confusion as to which "her" he meant, —Laura?

Gígja? someone else?—since many did not know where their leader had just been. There was a momentary awkward silence. It was broken at the sound of a great horn blowing from the cliff above. Laura was completely forgotten by Siklingur. He leaped out of his chair, knocking aside the servant who had returned with rags and was dabbing gingerly at his bloodied throat. He ran, followed by his warriors, advisors, and many others to the gates of the Great House. He and the many villagers looked to the cliff to see what was going on. There were Arnþor and his warriors standing tall and proud above them. One of Arnþor's men held forth a large flag. Siklingur, upon seeing people who had arrived from the same village as Laura, was more furious than ever. He ignored the flag, which signified the other party wished to negotiate peaceably, and shouted, "KILL THEM ALL!"

His warrior leaders began to yell, "ALERT! ALERT! GATHER! GATHER ALL WARRIORS! PREPARE FOR BATTLE!"

Most of the village's warriors and townspeople had already begun streaming out of houses and shops when they heard Arnþor's horn, signaling their arrival. Many went to collect their battleaxes, shields, armor, and weapons, then returned, ready to fight for the village and its people, and most importantly, Siklingur. The leaders moved down from the gates to coordinate the attack. They were shouting orders, getting their people in place and armed, when they heard a loud rumble of thunder. Everyone froze and looked up, puzzled. But the rumble was not coming from the sky—it was coming from the road into the village. The sound got louder and louder and the ground began to tremble beneath their feet. While the people were still standing there, trying to figure out what was going on, arrows began to fly into the village from the hillside around it. This caught everyone off-guard. Many of Siklingur's warriors were hit on the first salvo and fell, screaming, arrows sticking out of their torsos. Then the Hornafjörður appeared. The stampede hit the town like an explosion. Three hundred horses came galloping through the streets, mowing down everything in their path. Total mayhem ensued. People scattered, running and screaming, trying to get out of the way. Many could not move fast enough and were crushed. Others dove out of the way in time. Siklingur's warriors ran in all directions and found cover. They began firing arrows and hurling spears at the horses and toward the hillside when they could see the movement of their attackers. Several horses were hit and injured; they stumbled and faltered, but were able to keep going. A few staggered and fell.

Children screamed, women cried, the elderly moaned in despair, men cursed, sheepdogs barked and whined, and even mice, disrupted by the violent movement, ran along the streets, trying to escape. Vendors' carts were upended, their fruit and vegetables spilled out and smashed. The imprints of thousands of horses' hooves marked the streets and bodies were scattered about, trampled.

At this point, Arnþor's troops had disappeared from the top of the cliff and were charging around to the road. Emily, who had met up with Andrea and the warriors who had been assigned to them, leaped out of their hiding place as soon as the last of their horses thundered by and raced to follow them into the village. Once they were in the streets of the village, they used the pandemonium to act as cover as they scrambled to the gates of the Great House. The girls ducked into the small side streets, following Prinsessa's directions, gradually working their way closer to the Great House. All around them, chaotic noise echoed wildly—a baby crying, a man shouting, and the anguished yip of a dog in pain. Emily felt her heart beating a million miles a minute and could hear her breath amplified in her ears. Andrea had a stitch in one side and pressed her hand against it, but didn't slow down.

"Look out!" Emily yanked Andrea into a doorway, barely avoiding a large iron kettle that was flung out a window at one of the opposing warriors. It clanged loudly as it hit, rolling to a stop at the edge of the street.

The stampede of horses continued racing through the streets of the village, preventing the villagers from congregating anywhere. Confusion reigned while the noise thundered and the dust swirled. It was blinding and deafening all at once.

Meanwhile, Prinsessa and Hela cantered into town with Kim and Darcy clinging low to their necks, trying to make themselves invisible. The rampage of horses was a coordinated effort, and as soon as the horses saw Prinsessa and Hela, they opened a way for them. The girls could hardly register anything they passed. They kept their heads so low, they could not see much. Within minutes, they had gotten around to the back of Siklingur's Great House. This area was isolated from the total confusion in the town. They could still hear noise, but it was muffled.

Darcy and Kim jumped off their horses and took a few steps, catching their breaths and getting their equilibrium back. "Whew, that was something!" Kim exclaimed and Darcy nodded with enthusiasm.

Siklingur had run back into the Great House to take refuge with his personal warriors and direct the attack. They gathered in one of the interior rooms of the Great House, away from windows, everyone talking at once.

Finally, Emily and Andrea made it to the gates of the Great House. They were attacked immediately. Prinsessa was just starting to help Kim and Darcy as they put their plan in action, but she was pulled away to the more immediate threat Andrea and Emily faced. As soon as they hit the first step of the Great House, Prinsessa conferred upon them the same powers she had given Laura. Siklingur's warriors raised their spears, bows, and swords, but hesitated. Before them appeared two youthful looking females awkwardly draped with ill-fitting clothing and armor—how could this be? What kind of warriors look like children in costumes?

It was a dreadful violation of the warriors' honor to kill women. Doubt flooded their minds. As the warriors wavered, the two girls began to glow with a golden radiance. Lit up from within, they transformed from regular looking teenaged girls to able-bodied, powerful warriors. Their faces glowed with confidence and determination, their hair shone in golden clouds and the muscles in their forearms turned ropy and strong. With a flourish, Emily and Andrea unsheathed their swords and began to parry with powerful strokes against the seasoned warriors. More of Arnþor's warriors appeared to join them and Siklingur's army came to their senses. The battle was on. The clang of the swords, the yelling of the men, encouragement shouted among the girls, and the thunk! of a body falling filled the air. Back to back, Emily, Andrea and Arnþor's warriors fought their way through the gates and into the Great House. Once inside, Arnþor's men held Siklingur's fighters back, while the girls and three warriors followed Prinsessa's directions through the house and down the wide hallways to where Laura was being held. Holding their swords in an offensive position, they never faltered, although Andrea panted, "Oh, darn it! Look, they ripped my sleeve!"

"You! I got blood all over me!"

"Yeah, you spattered some on me too—I'm better at jumping back than you!"

Servants and slaves in the house gasped and shrank back as the two came running through the hallways, swords flashing, their bodies still glowing from within. The workers did not know what to think of the golden figures moving down the hallways. Several crossed themselves, others wondered if they were seeing ghosts, one fell to her knees and bowed her head to the floor.

Prinsessa guided them right to Laura's door. Three of the warriors proceeded to bash the door in. Laura, hearing all the commotion, had gotten up and held both her sword and knife at the ready.

"Laura, oh, thank God, you're all right!" Emily ran to Laura and threw her arms around her friend.

"I am so glad to see you!" Laura barely got out before Andrea flung her body at the two and joined in the embrace.

"Prinsessa got us here!" Andrea told her.

"You wouldn't believe what's going on out there!"

"We fought like real warriors!" Andrea said with pride.

"What the heck were you thinking…going off by yourself like that? Oh!" Emily remembered. "Reynir's out there—boy, is he upset! He'll be so glad to see you!"

"I'll be glad to see him too!" Laura grinned and all three giggled.

Finally, the three girls got over their initial giddiness at finding each other and turned together to face the warriors who had come with them. They were shocked to see all the warriors on their knees. A mirror on the opposite wall showed them the reason. The three girls stood side by side with the image of powerful female warriors and a heavenly aura surrounding them.

"Look at you—you look like you got nuked!" Emily giggled, admiring Laura's golden glow.

"Yeah, you look like a human light bulb!" Andrea added.

"Well, so do you—wow, that is some powerful mojo!" Laura laughed, then sobered. "Okay, back to business. We've got to go get Gígja now."

They pushed through the crowd of more than twenty of Arnþor's warriors who had gathered. Some had come down from the mountain and fought their way in, and others were from Arnþor's personal troop. The girls headed down the cavernous hallway. Arnþor led the battle out in the square in front of the Great House, fighting alongside his warriors. As they rushed through the passages, Emily called out to Prinsessa.

"Prinsessa, we have Laura. Can you guide us to Gígja?"

"Yes, I am proud of you for reaching Laura," Prinsessa responded, since she already knew of Laura's rescue. "But do not worry about Gígja," she told them, "there are bigger problems ahead of you. I will deal with Gígja."

Prinsessa was right. As the girls reached the end of the hallway, they stopped short. Standing at the opposite end of the hall on the other side of a large common area was Siklingur and at least forty of his warriors. Laura did not hesitate—with a loud shout she pulled her sword and charged at the opposing line. Siklingur's heart stopped. He could not retreat with his warriors standing there—he would look like a coward! Emily, Andrea, and all of Arnþor's warriors followed up with their own yells and followed Laura into the fight.

·········

Meanwhile, Kim and Darcy had located the wood chute with Hela's help. Looking around to make sure the coast was clear, Kim dropped her body armor and helmet on the ground.

"What are you doing? You won't have any protection!" Darcy looked at the pile.

"Well, first of all, we won't fit through this opening. And even if we take it with us, we can't move very well, or very quietly, in all this stuff. We've got to leave it behind," Kim told her.

"Okay." Darcy turned around and stood blocking her, trying to look nonchalant in case anyone wondered what they were doing. Kim pushed open the small door and carefully stuck her head in, her ponytail falling forward over one shoulder. Her neck was bent at an awkward angle as she tried to peer around. She lay there for a moment, listening to see if she could hear anyone nearby.

"What are you doing?" Darcy asked in a loud whisper, looking at her friend lying prone on the ground.

"Sh-h!" Kim's head came part way back out. "I'm making sure there's nobody waiting to grab me in there!"

"Oh, good thinking. Sorry, Kim," Darcy fell silent.

"It's okay, just give me a sec."

Hearing nothing, Kim squeezed her way into the chute, wiggling a little and when most of her body weight was through the door, gravity took over and she fell onto the woodpile with a muffled oomph! She got to her feet, covered with wood chips, her ribs and one arm bruised from the hard edges of the wood, picking a couple of splinters out of her arms. She stayed close to the stone wall, not wanting to be out in the open. A large spider, disturbed by the shifting wood, scuttled away and Kim shuddered. She wouldn't mention it to Darcy. She leaned out and peered down the passageway in both directions. Lit by candle wall sconces, to the left was a door and large storeroom, filled with barrels, shelves, and crates. A stairway led up from the passage where Kim was standing. To the right extended another long passageway with many doors, and Kim knew Gígja was behind the last door on the right. Her heart quickened with excitement. It was quiet down in the dungeons and the air was cool, dank, and, still.

"Is it okay?" Darcy said through a crack in the chute.

"Yeah, I think so, come on down—wait, come backwards and I'll guide your feet down," Kim told her.

Darcy, having also shed her equipment, lay on her stomach, pushing the door open with her feet, and skooched backwards. Once she was half way in, Kim grabbed her legs and helped her down the rest of the way, so her friend didn't land as awkwardly as she had.

Darcy got her footing and straightened her clothes, brushing off the dirt and smoothing her hair, looking around with curiosity.

"We've got to be really quiet, because we don't want any of the other prisoners to raise the alarm on us," Kim whispered.

"Let's use hand signals when we can," Darcy whispered back and Kim nodded back. "Good idea. Now, c'mon, there are the keys hanging right there!" The two were careful to cautiously look in all directions. Then Kim motioned for Darcy to go ahead and get the keys off the hook. She pantomimed holding them so they didn't jingle and make noise.

Darcy could feel her heartbeat pounding in her throat as she snuck along the side of the wall and reached for the keys. However, no one was there, because everyone was caught up in the many battles going on somewhere above their heads. Grinning at each other, Kim and Darcy ducked down low and headed for Gígja's cell. They unlocked the door and threw it open. Sitting on a bench against the wall was the beautiful daughter of Arnþor. She rose to her feet.

Kim and Darcy stood for a moment, staring at her. Throughout Gígja's captivity, Siklingur had ordered that Gígja was to have water to wash with and fresh clothing provided, luxuries not afforded any of the other prisoners. She was a beautiful girl, dressed in a sky blue flowing silk gown with an empire waistline and soft beaded slippers. She was slim and graceful, her hands white and thin, pale skin with spots of rose on her cheeks, a thin nose and high cheekbones. Her eyes looked like a female version of Arnþor's, a distinctive hazel color with flecks of greenish brown in the irises. Her cornsilk colored hair had been crudely styled; it was caught up and back in several places.

Gígja broke the younger girls' admiring looks by stepping forward, her hand reaching out to them.

"What is happening?" she asked, seeming unfazed by two twelve-year old girls dressed in trousers, tunics, and knee-high moccasin boots flinging open the door to her cell. She had been expecting something to happen after her encounter with Laura.

Kim said breathlessly, "Come on! We have to get out of the Great House! There are many battles going on above!"

"Believe me," Gígja told them, her eyes twinkling with humor, "I want to get out of here, the sooner the better!"

Without hesitating, she grabbed the keys Darcy was clutching and said, "Follow me!"

Gígja ran to the first occupied cell and unlocked the door, then the next and the next, and the next. Kim and Darcy both stepped forward, mouths open to protest, "What are you doing?" then realized Gígja knew exactly what she was doing. She was gathering recruits. Most of the men locked up in the cells were from Hólar. As soon as they saw Gígja, they thanked her profusely.

"Oh, daughter of Arnþor—thank you! I owe you my life!"

"Oh, blessed daughter, thank you! Thank you!"

"Yes, yes," Gígja replied. "Come along, now, quickly! Quickly!"

A line formed behind her. The men were thin and beaten, tired and hungry, dressed in ragged clothing and barefoot. All smelled terrible.

Since any key on the ring of keys would open any door, Kim got a key for herself and one for Darcy and in a few minutes all the doors in the dungeon had been opened. They shut all the cell doors behind them so it would not be obvious at first glance that they were all empty.

"Follow me!" shouted Gígja. She ran to the room where Kim had seen boxes, crates, and barrels stored and began pushing them over. Once again Kim and Darcy were confused, but understood after a minute or so when a box Gígja pushed over broke open and swords and knives spilled out of it. Mice scurried out of the way. The men grabbed the weapons in a wild free-for-all and then headed for the stairs.

An unfortunate guard, who had been tasked to check on and guard Gígja's cell, came down the stairs and around the corner at that moment. He didn't get the chance to say a single word before he was speared through the heart with a sword. He fell heavily to the stone floor with a grunt.

"Aye, this one works!" the prisoner held up the sword and looked at it admiringly. Everyone laughed. Two men picked up the guard by the arms and hauled him, legs dragging, into the nearest cell.

"We enter the battle for Arnþor!" Gígja cried, holding her knife aloft.

"For Arnþor!" the other prisoners picked up the cry and charged up the stairs, with Kim and Darcy picking up the rear. All of the prisoners came, even those not from Hólar; Siklingur and his men had treated them horribly during their captivity and they were hungry for revenge and had even formed friendships with the others from Hólar.

As soon as Gígja and her recruits reached the main hall, they ran directly into the battle between Siklingur's and Arnþor's troops. In the midst of a sea of bodies thrusting, parrying, stabbing, falling, swords flying, Gígja could see Laura, Emily, and Andrea glowing with the intensity of the sun and fighting with such skill that warriors were dropping one after another.

Kim and Darcy burst up at the end of the line and stood in shock, their mouths dropping open as they stared at the spectacle.

"Pssst! Get over here!" one of Arnþor's younger warriors, hardly older than they were, recognized them and pulled them aside.

"You don't even have any armor or weapons! Hide behind these and stay out of the way!" The boy shoved them over to two large solid iron urns, and then he turned back to the swordfight.

Kim and Darcy took in the whole scene—blood was flying, bodies lay about, swords tinged in a cacophony of offensive moves and defensive rejoinders. Kim watched in wonder at her sister deftly swiping her sword back and forth, up and down. Her feet moved in an ancient rhythm, positioning themselves this way and that.

She, Andrea, and Laura were not untouchable—Emily's sleeve was torn and she had blood on her arm; Laura had the same on one of her legs, and Andrea's hair, dangling out of her helmet, had been hacked off so that it was several inches shorter than the other side. All were totally focused and concentrating on their opponents. Kim and Darcy looked in awe at the odd glow they gave off—what was that? Some powers the horses had given them? Kim suspected it to be so.

Reynir was near the entrance of the Great House, off to one side, fighting like crazy. Being a farmer's son, he knew how to wield a blade, but was not as skilled with the finer points of sword fighting, the intricacies of the footwork, and the moves, as the others. However, his fury in knowing that Laura was in there, held captive, gave him the will and the brute force and strength to power his way through the fighting. Rather than utilizing the artistry of fencing, Reynir plowed through the warriors, stabbing with one hand and delivering a crushing blow with the other. He was out of sight of the main pack of fighters, more on the sidelines trying to creep nearer and nearer to the entrance, ever closer to reaching Laura.

Meanwhile, Prinsessa bestowed her powers upon Gígja, who also began to shine with an eerie pale light that warmed to gold and lit her from within. She had taken only a knife from downstairs, but quickly grabbed a sword from a fallen man. She and her fighters attacked from the rear. Siklingur's warriors were caught by surprise at the unexpected wave of people who poured out of the dungeons. They were now outnumbered by Arnþor's men. Fueled by adrenaline and anger, the weakened prisoners fought with determination.

Gígja joined with Laura and they inched toward the center where Siklingur stood, surrounded by his best warriors. Laura reached the ring first and maneuvered her way into the middle to face Siklingur. When he saw Laura break through the ring, Siklingur's eyes widened and Laura saw his Adam's apple move up and down as he swallowed hard. She grinned. Siklingur's warriors turned to protect him, but Gígja and Emily who had followed Laura, attacked with a vengeance.

"Get him, Laura!" Andrea called over.

"Yeah, get that little pipsqueak!"

Laura laughed out loud and turned to face her foe.

Siklingur, though shaken by the girls' presence and unbelievable skill with their swords, was not unskilled with his own. As Laura came toward him, he brought up his weapon and in a single parry sliced across Laura's left arm. Undaunted by the blood that welled up and spilled off her forearm, Laura returned his blow with a strike of her own to his side. Siklingur bent for a moment in agony, then straightened up and looked at Laura with hatred in his eyes.

The two battled hard. Emily, Gígja, Andrea, and the warriors fought around them. Siklingur struck often and with all of his body weight. He was beginning to overpower Laura with his blows. He hit her sword with such force that the blow broke her wrist.

A burst of pain shot through Laura's body and she screamed. The sword began to slide from her hand. When they heard Laura's scream, Emily, Gígja, Andrea, and the warriors they were fighting, stopped and turned toward the two. At the sight of Laura, bleeding, her face twisted in agony, Emily cried out, "Laura!" Andrea gasped and Gígja brought one hand up to cover her mouth.

Kim and Darcy hardly realized that they had stepped out from behind the planters into the open so they could see the drama unfolding in front of them.

As if in slow motion, every detail crystal clear, Siklingur brought his sword up for a final blow. The air was split by the loudest, most earth shattering yell coming from the depths of Arnþor's body. He had battled his way into the Great House. Shocked by the sight of the girls fighting, including his daughter, Arnþor let out the roar of a predatory lion. Siklingur turned his head, distracted for a moment. It was a fatal mistake. Laura, seeing Siklingur's hesitation, switched the sword to her left hand and lunged forward, driving the blade right up to the hilt into his chest.

"Your little bee has used its stinger well," she leaned forward and whispered into his face, his eyes opened wide and staring at her in horror.

She let go and Siklingur fell forward onto the ground, the sword jamming all the way through his body, the shaft buried inside him.

~ FIFTEEN ~

Peace at Last

As Laura watched Siklingur slide to the floor, dead, she began to feel her own knees giving out as darkness clouded her vision. Gígja, who had just knocked an Akureyri warrior backwards, turned her head just in time to see Siklingur falling with Laura's sword plunged through his heart. It appeared to Gígja as if it were happening in slow motion. Her mouth fell open as she watched Laura collapse on top of Siklingur.

"Emily!" Gígja called out. "Cover me!"

Emily gasped at the sight of Laura slumped over, but without hesitating, she stepped in front of Gígja and faced the warrior as he rose to his feet. Gígja turned and fell to her knees next to Laura's motionless figure. She pulled Laura off Siklingur, and laid her down, cushioning her head and brushing her hair back from her face.

"Laura! Laura, can you hear me?" she whispered.

By this time, her father had fought his way into the circle where Gígja sat and Laura and Siklingur lay. Arnþor stooped down, pulled open Laura's jerkin and put his head to her chest. After a moment or two he looked up into Gígja worried eyes and said, "She is alive, daughter."

Then Arnþor, reaching over Laura, threw his arms around Gígja and whispered in her ear, "My dearest daughter. I thank God you are safe."

Arnþor then stood up and shouted as loud as he could, "SIKLINGUR IS DEAD! OUR GREAT WARRIOR, LAURA, HAS SLAIN HIM! MAY PEACE REIGN AMONG US!"

The words echoed down the stony hallway but did not stop. The Hólar warriors picked up the news and shouted it out of the Great House and into the town. Almost immediately, the fighting stopped. Siklingur had held such power over his men that he had never allowed anyone else even to function as a second in command. There was no one who could replace Siklingur. Only a few had agreed with his evil practices and brutal methods of leadership. Certainly, there was no Akureyri warrior who had the bravery or the desire even to try to overthrow him.

Almost at once, first the Akureyri leaders, then the warriors put up their swords in a sign of surrender and then laid their weapons on the ground. A great cheer came from the Hólar warriors. Arnþor picked Laura up and stood.

Emily dropped her sword. It landed with a clang! and she

rushed to Arnþor's side. Andrea followed close behind her and hovered over her.

"How badly is she hurt?"

"I don't know yet. We will find somewhere to treat her. Come."

Arnþor, carrying Laura, went into the Great House, looking for a room with a bed upon which he could lay her. Emily, Gígja, and Andrea anxiously followed. The Hólar warriors solicited the help of those from Akureyri and together they began to attend to the wounded, both men and horses. Women and girls came out from hiding to help.

The Hólar warriors allowed the Akureyri warriors to pick up their weapons again as a sign of trust and willingness for peace between the villages. The dead from both sides, including both men and horses, were loaded onto wagons to be buried. The townspeople began to clean up the mess from the stampede. There was a feeling of relief and calm that settled over the village as soon as Siklingur was declared dead.

As Arnþor and his followers walked down the hall, Bishop Freysteinn, the bishop of Akureyri, approached Arnþor.

"Follow me," said Bishop Freysteinn, somber, his hands resting on his protruding stomach and over the richly brocaded robe he wore. "I will lead you to a place of honor where you may lay this honorable warrior." With fat fingers, he fingered the heavy silver cross that hung around his neck.

"She's not dead," Arnþor told him, "but she needs attention to her wounds and rest."

"Praise the Lord!" said the bishop. "Truly, He has watched over the angels who He sent to help you." Laura still had the golden aura surrounding her. "Come, Leader of Hólar."

Arnþor and the girls followed the bishop to a large room with beautiful furnishings and a big bed. Arnþor carefully laid Laura on the bed and Emily and Gígja removed her jerkin, weapons, and boots. Gingerly, they moved her broken wrist, laying it across her body. Andrea brought over a bowl of water and cloth for them to wipe the blood from the large cut on her arm and the sweat from her skin. The bishop went to get someone with medicinal skills while Arnþor stood over the girls, radiating pride and admiration.

"I believe the bishop was right," said Arnþor putting his arms around Gígja. "You are angels the Lord has sent to help us. There is nowhere else you could have come from."

Emily and Andrea stood up and turned to look at Arnþor and Gígja.

"Well, I wouldn't exactly call it heaven," Andrea said respectfully, "but we were brought to help."

Just as she said this Kim and Darcy came running into the room. They ran up to the bed, both looking ready to burst into tears at any moment, staring at Laura.

Gígja pulled away from her father's embrace and dropped to her knees behind the girls.

"You have saved my life," she said and both Kim and Darcy

turned around, surprised to see Gígja kneeling before them. Gígja took a hand from each of them and kissed them, and then she stood up and gathered them into her arms.

Both Kim and Darcy were quite embarrassed by Gígja's effusive thanks, and patted her back saying, "It's okay. We're just glad you're all right."

At that moment, Reynir came running in the door, looking disheveled, his jerkin sliced open at an angle and his blond hair wild and tangled.

"I was fighting around the corner and did not know where you had taken her," he blurted, moving frantically in Arnþor's direction. He elbowed Emily and Andrea aside, his hands reaching for Laura's face and hair, touching her softly.

"Laura, Laura, my Laura," he murmured.

"Be careful, her wrist is broken," Andrea told him, looking at the unnatural angle of Laura's hand and wrist.

"Yes," Reynir bent over her, kissing her forehead and murmuring in her ear. The others looked away as he kissed her soft lips, trying to will her back to him.

Laura lay motionless, her eyes closed, the aura around her still glowing and now encompassing Reynir.

Meanwhile, Emily had stepped over to hug her little sister and Darcy as well, relieved that the younger girls were all right.

"What happened to Laura?" Darcy asked, worried. "We heard she killed Siklingur, but she's not dead, is she?"

"No," replied Emily, "she has some cuts and bruises, and her wrist is broken, but she's alive. She must be exhausted as well. Laura has had a long day. She is truly a heroine."

Suddenly, Kim gasped and pulled away from her sister. She felt an idea forming and closed her eyes, concentrating. She called in her mind, "Prinsessa! Prinsessa!"

"Yes, my child," came the somewhat weak reply.

"What's wrong? Are you all right, Prinsessa?" Kim frowned.

"I was wounded with an arrow," said Prinsessa, in pain, "but some warriors are here and they will treat all of us who are injured. I am sure they will help me as soon as they can. There are many injuries worse than mine. I am just a little weak from the loss of blood."

"Oh, no!" Kim blurted out, panicked.

"I will be all right, child. Do not worry," Prinsessa reassured her. She sounded so confident that Kim felt better.

"Prinsessa, we are glad you will be okay, but Laura is hurt," Darcy interrupted. "They sent for someone with medicinal skills, but I don't think that is the best thing for her. Can you help?"

"Call Aríel," Prinsessa stated with authority. "She has achieved great strength with her own skills now and she will be able to help."

Aríel had not been far off and had been searching for the girls when she heard the conversation.

"I am here, I am here!" she said, worried about Laura and wanting to use her powers again. "I can help. Let me see her mind."

Kim turned to the other girls and exclaimed, "Aríel is going to help!"

Emily and Andrea had been listening to the conversation and chorused, "We know!" but Arnþor, Reynir, and Gígja look confused.

"What are you talking about?" Gígja asked.

"Oh, Gígja, I'm sorry. Wait, you will see something amazing," Kim told her.

"I have seen many amazing things today," Arnþor muttered, looking at the girls' clustered before him, their clothes tattered and ripped, their ponytails hanging loosely, and the residue of the gold aura still emanating off them.

Meanwhile, Aríel, standing outside the gates of the Great House, focused her mind solely on Laura and pushed her powers as hard as she could. In their minds, the girls could actually hear her grunting with exertion. Everyone turned and stared at Laura. Reynir, Arnþor, and Gígja watched too, although they weren't sure what they were witnessing. Before their disbelieving eyes, the cuts and abrasions slowly begin to disappear and Laura's bruises began to fade, from the angry reddish-black to a lighter red, then to dark pink and finally, back to her normal pink/gold skin tone. Soon the swelling in her wrist went down and her arm reformed its natural smooth shape. Reynir's face paled and he staggered back a step from the bed. Then Laura opened her eyes.

Aríel let out a sigh of exhaustion and Prinsessa praised her, "Well done, daughter, well done. Rest now."

"Yes, Mother," Aríel replied weakly, sounding satisfied.

"Where am I?" Laura asked, sounding healthy and full of energy. The aura around her glowed more brightly. She sat up and threw her legs over the side of the bed.

Reynir, who had been staring at her in shock, his mouth open, recovered. "Laura! You're all right! Thank God!"

Laura looked up and saw him. Her face broke into a huge smile. "Reynir!"

With a shout of joy, he pulled Laura up off the bed and into his arms, picking her up, hugging her, and twirling in a circle. Laura laughed with joy. When Reynir set her down, he grabbed her face in his hands and kissed her.

While this was happening, Gígja and Arnþor looked on in wonder.

"She truly is an angel from heaven," said Arnþor.

"Well, not really from heaven…" Andrea started to say, "but we were sent…oh, never mind."

Turning from Reynir, Laura opened her arms and the other girls hugged her all together, relieved their friend was all right.

"Okay, now, somebody fill me in, what in the heck happened?" Laura demanded, running her hands through her long blond hair to smooth it. She sat back down on the edge of the bed, and Reynir sank down on the floor at her feet, holding her hand.

Andrea, rarely at a loss for words, started right in. "It was so cool, Laura! You were fighting Siklingur and he was winning, and then he swung his sword so hard it broke your wrist! But then Arnþor came in and shouted his arrival and Siklingur got distracted and you switched your sword into your left hand and drove it right through his heart!" Andrea jumped forward, her arm out, pantomiming the final plunge of the sword with great drama. "You killed him! But then you passed out and you fell right on top of him! And we carried you here—well, Arnþor did—and Aríel healed your wounds," she forgot the fact that Arnþor and Gígja didn't understand the part about Aríel and she was not supposed to mention it.

Laura looked a bit bewildered by that whole explanation, although she got the gist of it.

"And we helped Gígja to escape!" Kim put in.

"Really? I want to hear all the details!" Laura told her, looking with pride at the two younger girls.

Arnþor said to Gígja, "Come, daughter. Now that we know Laura is all right, we have a lot of work to do. We must organize the leaders of the Akureyri warriors and find a suitable replacement for Siklingur. Then we must negotiate a final peace and make sure the town is in good order."

Gígja nodded. She took her duties as the chieftain's daughter very seriously.

Just as Arnþor was speaking, Bishop Freysteinn entered with a man carrying cloths, bottles of liquids, salves, and a wood splint. Arnþor turned to the bishop and said, "As you can see, those will not be needed. Laura was healed with powers and magic beyond our imaginations."

Freysteinn beamed. "Praise be to God! Ours is not to question His ways—we merely appreciate them. Without question, these are His heavenly angels," he said with conviction.

Andrea rolled her eyes.

The man carrying all the medical supplies stood frozen, staring at Laura in awe.

"However," said Arnþor to Freysteinn, "there are many others who are injured and need our help, so come, let us tend to them now. After we have seen to the wounded and the town has returned to order, we must set up a counsel of the Akureyri warrior leaders and select a new leader for Akureyri. Reynir, you have shown great courage and leadership today. You must come also and help us make decisions regarding these matters."

Obviously reluctant to let Laura out of his sight, Reynir basked in his praise.

"Yes, sir," he responded, squeezing Laura's hand and getting to his feet.

"I will see you as soon as it is possible, my Laura," he told her.

"Yes, they need you, but I will miss you," Laura reached up and kissed him lightly, then put her arms around his neck. Finally, they pulled apart.

Emily thought that if she were very lucky, someday someone would look at her the way Reynir was looking at Laura at that moment.

The four men and Gígja walked out of the room and left the five girls alone.

Rubbing her hands together briskly, Laura exclaimed, "I'm starved!"

"We all are," Andrea replied, "but let's clean up a little before we go out into the Great House. I feel gross." The other girls nodded. Everyone was dusty and sweaty, and their clothing was bloody from the battle.

"All right, but let's be quick! No futzing around. I can't remember the last time I ate—it was so long ago," Laura complained.

"Over here!" Darcy motioned, having checked out a doorway leading out of the bedroom quarters. It was a sort of bathroom— at least there was a kind of tub and water boiling over a fire. Earlier, one of the chambermaids had been instructed to come in a back passageway and stoke up the fire for hot water. Each girl took a quick turn in the tub using a mixture of hot water from the cauldron and cold water from a large barrel in the corner.

Everyone felt refreshed and rejuvenated. They shook out and brushed off their clothes as best they could, which did help, and combed out and redid each other's hair, braiding it or pulling it back. Using her knife, Laura was able to even out Andrea's hair, cutting one side (admittedly, a little unevenly) to match where one of the warriors had hacked it off on the other side. Finally, they put their weapons back on, and went out, ravenous, to look for food.

While Laura was being healed and the girls washing up, there was a lot of activity going on in the Great House. The hallways were cleared and swept down. People were running back and forth, on a variety of errands and missions. Laura grabbed one of the servants passing by and asked, "Excuse me, can you tell us where we can get something to eat?"

The woman looked at them, fearful, and bowed her head so Laura could hardly hear her reply. "Oh, great warriors from heaven. The counsel is waiting for you. There is food in the Great Hall."

"Geez! For the millionth time, we're not from heaven! We're from..." was all Andrea got out before Emily clamped a hand over her mouth and started dragging her down the hall.

Amused, Laura politely thanked her and the girls scampered down the hallway to the Great Hall.

"Andrea! You cannot say...."

"I know! But...."

"But nothing! Accept it! You have never in your life had anyone think you, of all people, are an angel from heaven! It might be your only chance! Enjoy it!" Emily scolded her.

"Well, when you put it that way..." Andrea grinned.

When the girls walked into the Great Hall, they saw a large group of people eating and drinking together in a loud and joyous celebration. Sitting at the huge table were Arnþor, Reynir, and

Gígja at the head, and warrior leaders from both Akureyri and Hólar.

When Arnþor saw the girls, he stood and said in a loud voice, "Stand for the warriors!"

Everyone in the room stood and began to cheer. Reynir stood with a mug of ale in his hand, and meeting Laura's eyes, he lifted the stein in her honor. Laura winked at him with a secret smile.

The girls, blushing a bit at all the attention, waved to everyone in the room and walked to the seats at the head of the table which Arnþor had saved for them. They reached for the food arrayed on platters on the table and dug in hungrily. There was a large selection of fish, plus some game birds that had been roasted, and lots of bread, fruit, and vegetables. Everything tasted wonderful.

Arnþor held up his hands and the room grew silent.

"Here is what I believe and I know many of you will agree with me. The Lord had decided that there needed to be peace between our villages and he sent these warrior angels to bring it to pass." Arnþor gestured to the girls and there was a murmur throughout the people, "Yes."

"Yes, it is so."

"Yes, it is as you say."

"Lord be praised for sending these warriors."

"It is our duty now to complete this task," the leader continued, looking around the room and fixing his gaze on first one person, then another. "No one in this room can deny what I say, now that you have seen them. The death of Siklingur was ordained and we must now choose a leader who will work with me to overcome the adversities and challenges of both our villages. Our greatest issues have been the fighting across our country and also the terrible problems we face due to the unusually severe weather, because it has affected our crops, our livestock, and our living conditions."

Again, there were murmurs and nods of agreement from everyone.

One of the Akureyri leaders stood up and said to Arnþor, "We all agree with what you say, but none of us has been prepared to take the place of Siklingur. He made sure of that. Perhaps we should make it the decision of the people to select Siklingur's successor." The man who had spoken was tall and powerful, a kind man. He was also popular with the people and though Siklingur had forbidden free speech, he was the most outspoken. Siklingur would have put him to death for this if he had not been such a good warrior. His name, Agnar, meant "disciplined warrior."

"You speak wisely," replied Arnþor. "I also believe we should let the people of Akureyri choose from one of you. After we have eaten, we will go to the gates and call everyone together. Then we will let the villagers decide."

A cheer went up from the table and the warriors went back to eating and celebrating. The bishop, sitting on Arnþor's right side, spoke softly to him of ideas he had for the two villages to work together. Arnþor listened, leaning to one side, and nodding occasionally

The girls wolfed down their food and water and even had a few sips of mead. Darcy and Kim tasted it and made faces. "Yuck!"

Laura managed to eat one-handed, since she and Reynir were holding hands under the table and didn't want to let go.

After they had eaten all they could, Emily spoke up.

"Arnþor, do you have other duties for us or may we go and check on our horses?"

"Oh, of course, you are free to see to your horses," he told her kindly. "We will be here a while making arrangements and decisions."

"Thank you, Arnþor!" Darcy and Kim stepped over to hug him and Gígja. Andrea and Emily smiled at him, and Laura squeezed Reynir's hand and brushed his cheek briefly with hers before rising.

As the five girls left, the entire gathering stood and toasted them. The applause and cheers followed them down the hallway.

"Prinsessa! We are coming to you. Where are you?" Emily called. Prinsessa responded and the five of them ran out to the small pasture where men were working to treat the injured horses. They found Prinsessa, Aríel, Kedja, Skessa, Hela, and Kafteinn gathered around Prinsessa. She was lying quietly as a man was removing an arrow from her side. Kim ran up and placed Prinsessa's head on her lap as the other girls each threw their arms around their own horses. Kim had tears in her eyes as she asked Prinsessa, "How bad is it?"

"Oh," Prinsessa told her soothingly, "not bad. As soon as this man removes the arrow, I can heal the wound myself."

"I healed your wounds!" Aríel told Laura with pride.

"And you did an excellent job," Laura kissed Aríel on the nose. "I'm so proud of you!"

By this time, the man had removed the arrow, which had penetrated Prinsessa's muscle, but, fortunately, none of her vital organs. In a moment, Prinsessa rose to her feet. The villager treating her turned to get some cloth bandages and salve, but by the time he had turned back around, the wound was completely healed. His mouth dropped open in surprise.

"What... How...?"

"Why are you surprised? That horse belongs to one of the warrior angels. Their powers reach beyond us," another man treating the wounded horses told him.

"Ah, yes, it is so."

"If only they knew the truth—that we aren't giving the horses our powers—it's the other way around!" Emily muttered to Laura, who laughed.

"Yeah, I don't know if they could deal with that."

"I feel like running," Prinsessa announced. "How about you?" she asked the other four horses. There was an enthusiastic response. Prinsessa said, "Hop on, girls. It has been an exciting day! Let's go for a run!"

The girls mounted their horses and took off at a canter, down to the beach along the fjord.

Kafteinn had followed and told them, "You girls have saved us all. Both villages will be better because of you. You will be held in great honor for all time."

"Thank you, Kafteinn, but just for a little while, we want to enjoy this and not think about it," Emily told him and he replied, "I understand."

"Let's go!"

Sand kicked up and water splashed around them in big sprays as they ran along the edge of the beach. Birds, hunting for prey along the water's edge, flapped off, startled by the ruckus the horses were making.

"Whee!"

"Whoo-hooo!" Darcy and Kim cried out with youthful exuberance, throwing their arms up in the air and feeling the power of the horses under their legs.

Andrea and Emily grinned at each other, laughing out loud.

Laura followed last on Aríel, joyfully closing her eyes and feeling the sun and the salt spray on her face, happy.

"You did it, Laura! I'm so proud of you!" Aríel told her.

"No, Aríel, we did it, and I am proud of both of us!" Laura squeezed Aríel with affection.

Kafteinn cantered along, enjoying the sheer pleasure of running with his longtime and far away herd members.

Eventually, they headed back to Akureyri. As the horses walked to the Great House, the girls saw that much work was yet to be done. Signs of death and destruction still remained. They hopped off the horses and gave them loving pats.

"I wish you a blessed good night," Andrea told Kedja, then added, "Hey, I'm getting pretty good at this language thing!"

"It's a different style of speaking than at home, isn't it?" Emily agreed, with an extra pat to Prinsessa, happy that her horse showed no signs of her previous injury.

The horses departed for the fields.

As soon as the girls went into the Great House, the bishop greeted them.

"I am glad to see you have returned, my angels from heaven."

Emily gave Andrea a warning look. Andrea scowled.

"We have been busy here, trying to put things to rights. Tomorrow the people will choose the new leader of Akureyri. Why don't you get some food and rest? We have a feast prepared in the East Gathering Room and beds have been readied for you," the bishop smiled.

"Thank you, bishop. That sounds...heavenly," Andrea said innocently, deliberately not looking at Emily, who couldn't help giggling.

The other girls murmured their thanks as well. Laura kept an eye out for Reynir, but didn't see him as they made their way to the room with all the food. As they snacked, Laura demanded all the details on what Kim and Darcy had done to get Gígja freed. Andrea and Emily also filled her in on what had happened when they discovered she had gone missing in Hólar and what had transpired from then until they got to her. The girls laughed and interrupted each other, rehashing every detail of the part they had played in the day's battle. Andrea glowed with happiness—she had never felt this close to her friends, or so accepted and liked.

Finally, they wound down and headed for bed. Servants led them to two adjoining rooms that had been prepared for them. Emily, Andrea, and Laura shared one room—it had two large beds with thick down comforters.

The identical adjoining room allowed Darcy and Kim to each have their own beds.

"Oh, my gosh, this quilt thing is so soft," Kim sank into it.

"Now, you guys go right to sleep and don't stay up doing a lot of laughing and talking—we need a good night of sleep," Emily fussed, tucking her sister in.

"We won't!" the girls chorused, looking at each other and giggling.

Emily went back to the other bedchamber, leaving the adjoining door open a few inches.

They were all so tired that everyone climbed into the high beds and fell asleep right away. Laura barely moved when Reynir came in, holding a glowing candle in one hand. He leaned over her and kissed her cheek, his lips warm on her skin.

"Mmm," she smiled in her sleep and woke up enough to realize he was there.

"I am sorry I woke you."

"I'm not. Why do you have a candle? The twilight provides plenty of light—it's a beautiful night," Laura whispered so she wouldn't wake Emily or Andrea.

"I wasn't sure how light it would be in here and I wanted to make sure I could see you," he told her.

"Yes, you might end up kissing the wrong girl," Laura teased in a sleepy whisper.

"There is no one I could ever mistake for you, ever, Laura, ever," Reynir told her intensely. "Now, go back to sleep," He kissed her properly, his lips soft against hers and then firmer, their breaths mingling, then he snuck back out. Sighing with pleasure, Laura rolled on her side and listened to Emily and Andrea's even breathing.

·········

Emily sat straight up in bed, awakened by great bells ringing and horns blowing. The call to the people had begun. She looked around, stretching, and saw that Andrea was stirring and Laura was up, stretching to look out the window and see what was going on. She peeked over through the adjoining door and made sure the younger girls were up and awake.

"What is that horrible noise so early in the morning?" Andrea groused. She sat up, her hair sticking up wildly on one side of her head.

"That, my dear, is the cause for celebration and the advent of a new leader for Akureyri," Laura laughed. "Let's get going."

Servants had taken their clothing, washed everything and sewn up all the rips and tears. It felt good to put on fresh tunics and trousers. They washed up and tamed Andrea's hair as best they could. Food had been laid out for them while they slept. They ate as they dressed and then hurried down to the gates of the Great House.

Several of the Akureyri warrior leaders were standing in a line beside Arnþor. A cheer went up when the girls arrived, but Arnþor, who had already begun his speech to the villagers, silenced it and continued speaking.

The Hólar chieftain was explaining to the people that it was up to them to choose their new leader from one of the warriors standing up beside him. He went to each man and held a hand above his head. For each one, polite applause or a small cheer came up from some of the people. When he came to Agnar, last in the line, the entire village exploded in cheers.

Arnþor turned to Agnar and said, "Congratulations, it is clear that the people desire you to be the Chieftain of Akureyri."

Agnar looked embarrassed for a moment, then straightened and shouted to the people, "I am honored and I will do my very best to serve you! We shall have peace with Hólar. Arnþor has said that he will help me to become the ruler you deserve!"

The people cheered. Arnþor and Agnar walked together back to the great hall followed by the warriors. They had much to discuss.

Now the girls had a lot of time on their hands. Arnþor and the Hólar warriors decided not to return home until the next day. Even Gígja played a major role in the planning and discussions of the counsels. The girls pitched in to help the people restore the village. When they needed a break, they rode up and down the fjord and into the mountains, marveling at the beauty of the lands around Akureyri. The wide fjord shone with the reflection of the sun as it traveled out to sea. The snow-covered mountains appeared to touch the heavens. At first glance, the river valley appeared flat and unremarkable, but as the girls cantered along, they saw tiny flowers sprouting up between the rough grasses. Field mice and birds initially scattered at their approach, but then would stop to watch them pass. Huge lava fields flowed down from ancient volcanoes like dark rivers. Mighty glaciers, iridescent blue, rested in the passes between mountains far up the valley.

Arnþor needed Reynir's help, so Laura didn't see him all day.

She understood his responsibilities and felt proud of him, but missed being able to spend time with him. She grew anxious, knowing their time together was limited. She had never felt this way about a boy.

Emily, Andrea, and the younger girls' antics distracted her and she enjoyed the day, in spite of her worries.

That night, they all took hot baths and washed their hair. It felt good to be clean again.

While everyone slept, Reynir again crept into the bedchamber, candle in hand. This time, Laura got up and they went out into the deserted passageway.

"It is so good to see you," Reynir set the candle down and gathered Laura in his arms.

"You too. I missed you today. But you look tired," Laura frowned, pulling back and looking into his face.

"Yes, it has been a long day, but we accomplished much," he threaded his long fingers through Laura's silky loose hair and drank in her face. "It is wonderful to know that the fighting among our villages has ended and we can all live in peace now."

"I'm so glad," Laura told him, reaching up and kissing his jaw. His arms tightened around her. "You're my very favorite warrior," she teased.

He kissed her senseless.

"Now, get back to bed and I better do the same," he told her, "unless there's room in there for me..." he gestured toward Laura,

Andrea, and Emily's room.

"Yeah, right," Laura laughed. "Go on, I'll see you tomorrow."

"It was worth a try," Reynir grinned. He kissed her softly and said, "There is nothing I would like more than to hold you in my arms all night. Good night, sweet Laura."

For the second night in a row, Laura fell asleep smiling.

· · · · · · · · ·

The next day, Arnþor and his daughter, the warriors, and the girls gathered at the edge of the village to make the return ride to Hólar. Friends had been made between the villagers. They bid each other a fond farewell. The people of Akureyri cheered and waved their goodbyes as those from Hólar rode away.

Arnþor took his time riding back to Hólar. He stopped a few times for rest and food and sometimes tölted just for the pleasure of it. Andrea, Emily, Darcy, Kim, and Gígja rode together, talking and laughing the whole way. This time, Andrea rode in the middle of the group, between Emily and Gígja. They shared their excitement of the battle and Gígja's escape. Gígja told them of her life and plans for the future.

"What about you?" Gígja asked them.

The girls remained silent for a moment, trying to decide what they could say, remembering Prinsessa's warning not to speak of their lives at home.

Finally, Emily spoke. "We have many of the same wishes that you do for a happy life, families and friendships, and enjoying our horses. We are lucky to have each other and mostly, we are just enjoying being here and the experiences we've had together."

Gígja nodded.

Laura and Reynir rode a bit behind them, sometimes talking, sometimes not, relishing having the whole day to spend together. They held hands when they could as Laura admired the beautiful scenery.

"See? That is another good thing about your being here—you see things in a whole new way," Reynir told her with admiration. "I have looked at these same mountains and fjords all my life and not really noticed how beautiful they are until you pointed them out. It is a beautiful place to be. I see that now."

Laura smiled at him, nodding in agreement.

Finally, the army arrived home and the streets came to life with people cheering for the return of the warriors and the news of peace with Akureyri. That night, a great feast was held in the Great House. Food and music were enjoyed throughout the town. The entire village welcomed Gígja back with great fanfare and joy. Reynir spent most of the evening in the midst of his large extended family that surrounded him with pride. They all wanted to celebrate their own hero. He and Laura realized it would be difficult for them to be together right then and accepted it, going their separate ways during the party. They had spent the whole day together, and Laura also wanted to celebrate with her friends.

Darcy, Kim, Emily, Andrea, and Laura were toasted and honored so much that they finally broke away and found a quiet section of the town away from the music and food, where they could just be with their horses. Andrea, Laura, and Emily were now the best of friends and Kim and Darcy had enjoyed every moment of the adventure. They all knew on some subconscious level that it would have to come to an end, but everyone pushed the thought aside and just concentrated on the celebration at hand.

~ SIXTEEN ~

Returning Home

Once back in Hólar, the girls continued to avoid the thought of going home. They realized they had been given a reprieve when Prinsessa didn't mention leaving. Instead, for a few days they spent time riding out into the countryside, investigating the village and the Great House more thoroughly, and getting better acquainted with the people in Hólar.

They received much honor from the people who treated them like royalty. The girls tried just to ignore this and after a while, the villagers gradually became more comfortable around them.

However, Prinsessa kept the golden aura around them—she liked it and it set them apart. Strangely, the girls had begun to feel at home here. They had moved into the Great House with Arnþor and Gígja. Their weapons and jerkins had been hung in a hall of honor with those of Arnþor's ancestors. They now wore women's clothing, dresses and gowns, made of fancy brocades and silks, and soft slippers on their feet. They wore girls' riding clothes as well as more casual cotton and linen dresses for day wear. Privately, Emily and Laura agreed that they did miss wearing jeans and tennis shoes. Handmaids fashioned their hair into crowns of braids or piles of curled masses.

Gígja spent a lot of time with them, especially when they rode. She showed them the lands around Hólar and they made several trips down to Akureyri and the sea. The girls enjoyed learning more and more about the people, customs, and general way of life. Of course, the horses were a big part of the fun. Hela, Kedja, and especially Aríel were having as much fun as the children. They took the girls to see the great herds of Hólar. Emily and Kim had to select different horses to ride from the herds of Hólar because Prinsessa, Skessa, and Kafteinn spent most of their time in deep and important discussions. If fact, Arnþor picked out two of the best horses in his personal herd and presented them to Kim and Emily. It didn't take them long to become good friends with the new horses.

Laura spent most of her time with Reynir. The two traveled together, ate together, and often went off on their own together. Aríel was happy for Laura. She had never been able to feel true love through a human before, but her bond with Laura allowed her to actually feel what Laura was feeling for Reynir. This warm and enjoyable feeling showered down on her as they rode.

Reynir was in denial about Laura's time there coming to an end.

He tried to hide his anguish from her so he didn't ruin their time together. He had never met a girl like her before, and felt that she was the one true love of his life. He did not want to think about how empty his life was going to be without her in it. Laura sensed the desperation in his kisses, but there was nothing she could do to change it, so she just tried to make every moment count.

In their minds and memories, the girls' real homes and families had grown faded and blurry. Emily suspected Prinsessa was responsible for that, and acknowledged it was probably easier this way. She vowed to enjoy the time they had now, and accept the fact that it couldn't last forever, and all would be fine when they finally went home Meanwhile, Prinsessa, Skessa, and Kafteinn spent all their time together. The success in the war between Hólar and Akureyri was great, but it was only a small piece in a tumbling avalanche of problems the country now faced. Iceland had been a peaceful country, the first in all of Europe to establish a Parliament. Things had gone well for the last 300 years, but now a change was in the air. Kafteinn was sure it was the change in climate. The whole country was affected: the lack of food, deforestation, and other problems were causing battles and fights to pop up among other villages. The Parliament was trying hard to stop the problems from escalating, but the chieftains were becoming independent and power hungry. The horses knew how it would turn out because they had the ability to communicate into the future, as they had done with Prinsessa. By 1262, the King of Norway would take control of the country and they would not get their freedom back until 1944. Iceland faced 682 years of foreign control. This all was irrelevant and unchangeable. Although the horses were aware of future events, they were powerless to change them. Instead, they tried to strategize different ways to prevent harm from coming to the horses and the people. The three talked of things happening all over the country for almost three days, day and night, making plans and suggestions.

Finally, they had discussed every possibility. One afternoon Prinsessa and Skessa called the girls to the field near the Great House. They stood in a semi-circle with Kedja, Hela, and Aríel.

"The time has come. We must return home," Prinsessa announced.

Laura turned her head, her stomach dropping. She struggled not to burst into tears. Aríel moved to her side to comfort her.

"Reynir," she whispered.

"I know, Laura, I know," Aríel laid her head on Laura's shoulder.

"But Prinsessa," Kim, protested, who was also upset, "we haven't had enough time here! There is so much to see and learn and we're having such a good time. Do we have to go?"

"Our purpose here," Prinsessa reminded the girls in a serious tone, "was not to have fun. It was to rescue Gígja and bring peace to Hólar. We have accomplished those things. You girls were the key to the success of those two goals, but you cannot stay here forever. It is time to go home."

All the girls looked at their feet, silent. They all knew this was coming, and needed a few minutes to adjust to the news. Every one of them had changed, Andrea in particular, even without the magic of Prinsessa. She saw clearly now how foolish she had been before she had come to Iceland. She now understood true friendship and what really mattered in life. Thinking about how important her image, her expensive clothes, tack, and makeup were to her before made her feel ashamed for being so shallow. She vowed to treat Star very differently once she was home, and to keep her friendships with Emily and Laura. She had no idea what would happen with Erica and Heather, but would try to see if they could all be friends together—real friends. Andrea felt that she had become a stronger person and promised to herself that she would stay that way, without being a spoiled brat.

All the girls had grown up a lot, Kim and Darcy too. Some of that maturity was bound to wear off when they went home, but not all of it. Both of the younger girls had contributed during the journey in a myriad of ways. They also understood responsibility and caring for others in a new way.

"We will leave tomorrow," Prinsessa stated. "Arnþor wants to throw a farewell banquet for you tonight. Then tomorrow morning we will retrieve your belongings from Reynir's family home and head back."

That night, the unforgettable gala took place. The girls danced and ate; they were toasted so many times, they lost count. Laura and Reynir spent the whole evening together dancing and talking. Emily often saw tears in Laura's eyes and felt sad for her. The gala lasted late into the night and when the girls finally went to bed, they could barely move.

The next morning came far too soon. Prinsessa awakened them. Silently, they washed and dressed for riding. There was food laid out for them but no one could eat much. Laura felt burdened down with sadness. When they came out of the Great House, they saw that the entire village had come to bid them farewell. They were showered with hugs and kisses. All of the girls teared up when Máttur and Daria hugged them as if they were their own children. Daria gave them a bag with food for the journey, patting each of their cheeks.

Finally, everyone mounted up and rode off, looking back and waving to all who had come out to say goodbye. Reynir, who looked as if he had not slept at all the night before, held Laura's hand tightly all the way to his family's farm. Kafteinn went along with them. When they arrived, Reynir retrieved the bundles and the saddles. The girls went in and changed to their jeans and T-shirts.

"Hey, these feel funny," Andrea said, tugging at her jeans.

"Mine too. Do I look fat?" Emily asked her.

Their clothes felt tight, but not because they had gained weight. All of them had built up muscles they never had before. This had nothing to do with Prinsessa's magic; they had earned these new muscles.

"It's a good thing denim stretches a little," Emily added.

"Gosh, look at Laura's arms!" Andrea exclaimed. Her biceps were cut, curved, and tight.

Laura gave her a weak smile, dreading the parting from Reynir.

When they came out they looked odd to Reynir, but he could still see the warrior-like girls under their strange dress.

The girls began saddling and bridling their horses. Laura looked at Emily.

"Go ahead, I'll get this," Emily gestured to Aríel's saddle, feeling sympathy for her friend.

Her eyes full of tears, Laura stumbled along with Reynir as he led her behind the house to say a last goodbye to her.

"Laura, Laura, I don't want you to go!" Reynir choked, pulling her close to him.

"I know, I don't want to go either," Laura wrapped her arms around his neck and started to cry. She tried to memorize the feel of his strong arms around her, his unique smell of linen and fresh grass, the softness of his tanned cheek against hers. "I feel like my heart is breaking," she sobbed.

"I have never met anyone like you, Laura, and I know I never will. I don't know how I'm going to face the days without you," Reynir told her, running his hands up and down her back.

"I know. There's just something between us, I don't know what it is," Laura cried.

Reynir took her head in his hands, feeling the heavy silk of her hair, closing his eyes, breathing her in. His lips met hers and they kissed with an urgency they hadn't felt before. He could taste the salt of her tears.

"Keep working hard and help Arnþor however you can," Laura gave him a weak smile. It was the best she could do.

"Laura," Prinsessa's gentle voice came to her.

"I have to go. Thank you for everything, Reynir," Laura looked into his kind and loving eyes, soaking in his handsome face.

"Come back, Laura, come back to me," Reynir's eyes were filled with tears.

"I hope so." Laura made herself pull away from him and they slowly walked back around to where Andrea, Emily, Darcy, and Kim were standing next to their horses.

They all stepped forward and hugged Reynir, thanking him.

Laura hugged him fiercely and kissed him one more time and then they all mounted up.

They were so used to riding bareback that the saddles, bulky and stiff, felt odd to them.

In a flurry of goodbyes, the horses and girls headed down the valley. Reynir stood watching them, his hand lifted in a sad farewell. Laura was crying so hard, she could hardly see. Kafteinn accompanied them.

As they walked, Prinsessa began to lecture them.

"Now girls, in some ways you have grown and matured on your own and these changes will stay with you, but other ways are related to my magic and those will not go back with you."

"What does that mean?" Kim asked, anxious.

"Well, for one thing, we will not be able to talk to each other as we do here."

"That's terrible!" Emily exclaimed. "Can't you use your magic at home so we can still speak to you in our minds?"

"I could," replied Prinsessa, "especially now that you have been here, but unfortunately, it's more complicated than that. You must never mention this journey to anyone. Not anyone, even your friends and parents. It's like home is for you now—things will seem kind of fuzzy and blurred, but you will remember. But keep in mind, I can wipe the memory from you if I have to. This is only among the five of you and will remain your secret forever."

"Prinsessa," said Andrea, "will we ever get to come back?"

"You have honored yourselves beyond anything I imagined," Kafteinn put in. "I hope Prinsessa will bring you back."

"If the occasion calls for it," said Prinsessa. "These journeys are not a vacation. They have a purpose, as you have learned."

"What about the time we have been gone?" Laura felt a flicker of hope that she would get to return and see Reynir again. "Isn't that going to cause quite a stir?"

"Do not worry. All will be well," Prinsessa spoke knowingly.

"I am very proud of you all for everything you have done and how you have behaved. You have also achieved the goal your mother wanted, Emily." She looked at Emily and Andrea riding side by side, the best of friends. "We will not be able to speak to each other, but you have learned to understand us better and will therefore be able to be aware of our thoughts in some ways like we are aware of yours."

The girls rode on in silence a little farther and then Prinsessa said, "Ah, we are here, Kafteinn. It has been a pleasure serving you and it is my hope that we will see you soon." The girls' ears perked up at this.

"Once again, I would like to convey my deepest thanks," replied Kafteinn. "The people of Hólar and Akureyri will not forget you. Farewell; blessed journey to you, my friends."

"Goodbye, Kafteinn!"

"Goodbye!"

"Thank you for everything, Kafteinn!" The girls called.

Prinsessa gave a respectful nod to Kafteinn and then turned the girls down the valley, which extended out into the sea.

"Well, before we go back—I want to say something!" Aríel blurted out.

"Go ahead, daughter," Prinsessa told her.

"Me too, me too!" the other horses chimed in.

"We had quite an adventure, didn't we, Laura? I'm so glad we were paired up together!" Aríel told Laura.

"I am too. Aríel, thank you so much for all you did to help me," Laura leaned forward and hugged Aríel's neck.

"It was my pleasure—you really accomplished some remarkable things, Laura—I'm glad I got to be a part of them. And my powers have improved a lot too!" Aríel exclaimed happily.

"Kedja, you were a wonderful horse, thank you so much," Andrea told her.

"You too, we both learned a lot, I think, on this trip," Kedja replied.

"Can I still come and visit? Emily?" Andrea asked, sounding almost timid.

"Of course you can!" Emily looked over at her with a smile.

"I would love that!" Kedja said.

"We sure did have fun, didn't we, Darcy?" Hela piped up.

"You bet—you were the perfect horse for me, Hela!"

Emily, Kim, Prinsessa, and Skessa all stood together, silent, filled with emotion.

Finally, Prinsessa, said, "I think we all know how we're feeling. There's no need to say anything."

Everyone nodded and the girls hugged their horses.

"All right, now, line up and follow me," said Prinsessa. Those were the last words they heard from her.

In the time it took for the girls to blink, the forest stood before them, a small opening in the midst of the trees, looking just as it had when they first arrived.

The girls rode single file onto the path and into the woods. At the end of the line, Emily looked back. Kafteinn stood watching them go, his muscular body strong and proud, shining in the sun, his head lifted high.

"Goodbye, Kafteinn," Emily whispered.

The woods were shaded and cool. They had not gone very far when the trail opened wider and they saw the campground. The clearing had several cabins tucked into the woods. Clothes hung out to dry on the line by one and a couple of dogs came running up to greet them. A field and barns with a paddock sat off to one side. The air was crisp and fresh, with the scent of barbeque wafting over from the outdoor cooking area. Two park rangers came out of their office, dressed in beige uniforms with dark green patches on the arms, smiling and greeting them.

"Hello, girls! You must be the Miller party! Did you have a nice ride?"

The girls stared at them in silence for a second, and then smiled and nodded hello.

"Uh, yes, thank you," Emily recovered enough to say. "I'm Emily Miller."

"Okay, great! You're right on time—your mother said you'd be arriving in time for dinner, so why don't you put your horses up and throw your gear in your cabin—let's see," the ranger consulted his clipboard, "cabin number three, right over there," he gestured.

No time had passed from when the girls had ducked out of the woods, had their wild and adventurous journey in Iceland, and ducked back into this world again. Everyone felt a little shell-shocked.

Subdued and quiet, they got their horses settled in the outdoor stalls and then went to the kitchen for dinner.

Darcy and Kim stared at their plates with the hot dogs, baked beans, and coleslaw. The food seemed strange compared to what they had been eating. Several other families dined at the communal tables and the chattering conversations sounded like gibberish to the girls, who ate in silence. Soon, the others at the table began asking them where they were from and about their horses, and gradually, the strangeness began to wear off. They entered into the conversation and started feeling more like themselves.

Laura, sitting at the end of the table, had a funny feeling in the pit of her stomach. Already, the sharp memories of Iceland had begun to fade. "I don't want to forget—don't let me forget," she told herself, thinking of Reynir, and wanting to remember every single detail about him. She vowed to work hard at recalling things so he would stay close to her.

"Us?" Andrea's voice broke through Laura's thoughts. "Oh, we've been friends forever!" She grinned at Emily, who smiled back at her.

"That's wonderful—there's nothing like having your best friends to ride with," a woman sitting across the table from them responded. "My girlfriends have helped me through some tough times, and I always knew I could count on them. Now I have that with my husband!" she gave him a fond smile.

The pain in Laura's heart was so strong, she had to look away.

After dinner, Darcy and Kim started yawning so widely their jaws were cracking. The older girls felt tired too, both physically and mentally.

"Can we have s'mores for breakfast?" Kim asked her sister, half-asleep already.

"We'll see," Emily told her, patting her on the shoulder.

The thin bunk mattresses weren't the most comfortable, but everyone fell asleep right away. Their light cotton pajamas, wrinkled from being stuffed in their saddlebags, were comfortable but felt strange to their skin.

In the morning they rose early, had their breakfast, and started right out on the trail.

They cantered and tölted the whole way as if they were back in Iceland. It felt very different from their trip into the park, where they had meandered and stopped a lot for breaks and rest. The length of the trail seemed like nothing compared to the distances they had traveled in Iceland. Because of the pace they set, they made it back much earlier than they were expected, so Emily dug her cell phone out of its pouch and called Karen.

"Mom?"

"Hi, honey!" Karen's familiar cheerful voice on the phone made

Emily choke up. She hadn't realized how much she had missed her mother.

"Ahem, yes," Emily cleared her throat. "We'll be at the trailhead in about a couple hours, I think—can you meet us?"

"Oh, sure, no problem. It's early—is everything all right?" Karen asked, frowning into the phone. Maybe things had not gone as she expected, and the girls had hightailed it back as fast as they could.

"No, no, no worries, Mom, everything's fine. We had fun."

"Okay, I'll let the others know and we'll be up to meet you." They hung up.

The parents arrived at the parking area a few minutes before the girls. They got out of the trucks and waited, chatting and leaning on their vehicles. Within a couple of minutes, the sound of pounding hoofs reached them as the girls came cantering down the hill to the truck. When they dismounted, their parents stared at them, shocked by their appearances. The girls looked stronger, healthier and most noticeably, the feeling of camaraderie between them was evident.

Emily hugged Karen so hard, she knocked the breath right of her. Kim was right behind her and although she hugged her mother with her same innocent enthusiasm, Karen held her younger daughter at arm's length, looking at her. Kim exuded a feeling of maturity Karen had not seen in her before.

"How was it?" Karen asked, looking at her closely.

"Oh, it was awesome, Mom—we had a great time!" Kim exclaimed.

Andrea walked right up to her mother, gave her a giant bear hug, and then grabbed the cigarette out of her mouth, threw it on the ground and stamped on it.

"Mother, I want you to quit these things. You are killing yourself and killing me."

Andrea's mother looked at her in amazement, flabbergasted at her daughter's show of strength. Andrea's commanding air left no room for argument. Virginia, somewhat weak in character anyway, could not think of a thing to say. She did a double take—had her daughter cut her hair? No, she must be imagining things.

It didn't take long to load the horses. During the ride home, Kim and Darcy talked and laughed the whole way, answering Jim and Karen's questions about the trail ride. They seemed to have forgotten the whole Icelandic adventure, Emily thought to herself. They didn't seem to be having any problems with worrying about saying anything about it by accident. In the back seat, Emily was quiet and just looked out the window, thinking how different the terrain was here. In the fields they passed, birds and butterflies flittered, a small family of rabbits hopped through the tall grass, bees clung to the heavy summer blossoms, cows looked up lazily, their jaws grinding their hay in a rhythmic steady chew. Emily thought it looked cluttered with the overhead telephone wires, clunky telephone poles, mailboxes—nothing like the clean open spaces, beautiful mountains, and sea cliffs where they had been. She sighed.

Once they were home, everyone helped unload the horses, tack, and saddle packs. Andrea told her mother to help and she did. Shortly after that, they all headed to their cars. As the families were leaving, Karen saw Andrea and Emily hugging each other goodbye as though they had been best friends for years.

After everyone had gone, Jim retired to his den and Karen and the girls sat around the kitchen table eating potato chips and drinking sodas.

"So, I get the impression that this journey was a success?"

Emily looked her mother in the eye. "Oh, Mom, you have no idea."

A second later, Emily and Kim cocked their heads. They could have sworn they heard Prinsessa laughing.

The End

THE ICE HORSE
ADVENTURES

BOOK 2

PRINSESSA'S MISSION

by

DOUG KANE AND CHRISTY WOOD

The villagers of Hólar face an unseen and ruthless enemy that threatens to destroy them forever. Tough times have hit the area; the mysterious loss of livestock draws a bleak future for them all. When their children start disappearing, and a brutal winter is fast upon them, the Icelanders know Kafteinn is their only hope. The captain of horses summons his descendants to return to thirteenth century Iceland and return peace to the countryside. As the Miller sisters return to Hólar with Darcy, Laura, Andrea, and new friend Erica, hope returns to the hearts of the villagers.

With time quickly running out, the twenty-first century teens determine to reunite with their beloved ancestors and take up the call once again. The horses and the girls face unforeseen danger and a terrible magic that may bring the end for them all.

Prinsessa's Mission—coming April 2009.
ISBN 978-0-9817234-1-9